no matching record

OF LOVE AND COURAGE

LISA HENNIGH
AND
LUISE BAGGETT

Copyright © 1997
by
Luise Baggett
1820 Woodview Drive
Alvarado, TX 76009

ISBN 1-886698-13-9

Library of Congress Catalog Card Number:
97-61818

DD 256 .H46

ACKNOWLEDGMENT

I am deeply grateful to my loyal friends Dr. Leon Abbott and his lovely wife Julie, a pearl of a woman. Because of their continuous encouragement and inspiration, I was able to write of the memories that had been buried in my heart for so long.

To my loving and tireless daughter and my best friend, Luise, who dedicated a tremendous amount of time assisting with the manuscript and making countless revisions for me, my very special thanks, as well as to my son-in-law Dennis Baggett for his endless patience.

I could not forget to acknowledge my one and only grandchild, Michael Justice. He is the greatest grandson a grandmother could want.

My love and heartfelt thanks to all of you.

Contents

PROLOGUE 1

CHAPTER 1 3

CHAPTER 2 16

CHAPTER 3 34

CHAPTER 4 53

CHAPTER 5 73

CHAPTER 6 79

CHAPTER 7 102

CHAPTER 8 105

CHAPTER 9 116

CHAPTER 10 126

CHAPTER 11 140

CHAPTER 12 162

EPILOGUE 174

FOREWORD

This compelling book, through the incredible talent of a mother-daughter team, intrigues the reader with the imponderable of what it really means to live. It is not only about love and courage but about learned optimism and harsh reality in a time of helplessness, pain and chaos. Their story is a story of an ordinary German family. Reading this book is like actually sitting across from Lisa and Luise and becoming engaged in an engrossing and compelling conversation with them. The remembrances are from the heart of someone who lived in the incredible times during World War II. The recollections that Lisa shares in this book have not only made my life more purposeful, but foster a greater appreciation for the many German families who risked all they had to help Jewish families during the Holocaust. You too should experience a deeper and richer understanding of how others did what they could in extraordinarily terrible times.

During the past few years, as this book was being written, I have experienced an increased awareness and appreciation for Lisa Hennigh. She has seen human misery and experienced living in a society which strangled the human spirit, wilted the faith and hope and created helplessness among the population. I have witnessed many of the tears as she relived her tumultuous past and shared laughter as she is quick to recall many of her fond childhood memories.

You will read about naiveté, love, passion, optimism, inspiration, fear, survival, and hope for the future. And in a fundamental way this book is about the application of the feelings emerging from this experience. As a friend, I have been touched by each of her incredible stories, but none touched me as deeply as the ones gripped by conflicting emotions. First deep remorse at the loss of her family and friends, then relief that the suffering was over, and finally the elation of having the privilege to know such a person.

Her objective in writing this book was to provide a mental panorama of events that permit the individual to place him or herself in the "big picture" prior to, during, and after the war. I believe she has achieved her objective in an outstanding manner.

Before closing, I should like to share with you her dedication of the book. I believe it is her sincere hope that no matter how much she regrets the past with all the human suffering, that *Of Love and Courage* edifies the reader with the fact that there were many wonderful and benevolent people willing to risk their lives to help their friends during the war.

A final word about the author, my friend and teacher. I bow in obeisance and in tribute to her and to her work. The book is a labor of love and a contribution to the world that would relieve in some way the suffering of others. It is from her experiences and her own wonderful gift of writing in addition to the talent and compelling style of her daughter Luise Baggett that this book has come to fruition.

The publication of this book comes in a time when the peoples of the world actively long for freedom and the chance to create a life that has both purpose and possibility, a life that has hope. Whenever life presents a new challenge or requires a change in course, it is my counsel that you remember the experiences so capably described in *Of Love and Courage*. I recommend this book to you.

Leon Abbott, Ph. D.

PROLOGUE

The jet engines roared then gradually changed into a high pitched whine as the plane made its steady ascent skyward. The clouds below resembled giant mounds of cotton. Lisl imagined one could almost jump up and down on them like some huge celestial featherbed. She looked over at her daughter Anita who was gazing out the window. Impatiently, Anita flicked a pen between her fingers as she waited for the seat belt light to go off so she could pull out her notepad and write again.

A sentimental journey, Anita called it — this trip that she and Lisl were taking. A trip through a vast tunnel of time was more like it, Lisl thought — this two week vacation in Germany, the place of their births. Anita had been interviewing her on-and-off for months now — determined to get her mother's story down on paper before she died, Lisl supposed. Although at sixty-nine, she had no plans to check out from this old world just yet. Her entire life story was what Anita wanted. Her daughter felt there was a message here. She wanted the world to know what it was like to survive the war from "the other side of the hill." The world already knew of that ignominious period in history where European Jews were exterminated in masses — the Holocaust as they now call it. Even after fifty years, Lisl's heart was still saddened whenever she read or heard of the ongoing hatred some Jews still felt towards modern-day Germans. She wanted the healing to begin. Her story, Lisl thought, will be different.

The reliving of those early years in her life for Anita's notepad brought back a bittersweet kind of memory, a kind of pain deep in

Lisl's heart that was almost unbearable at times. She wondered how this trip to actually see the places where it all happened would affect her so many years later.

"Are you ready to tell me some more?" Anita asked, her pen poised over notepad as the plane leveled off.

"Sure, where do you want to start?" Lisl asked as she settled back for the long, tedious flight.

"Well," the young woman said, "let's go back to the very beginning again. Tell me about *Opa*... you know, when you gathered mushrooms in the forest," Anita replied. She loved to hear stories of the grandparents, *Oma* and *Opa,* that she never really knew.

Lisl closed her eyes momentarily and allowed her mind to drift back again to a time so long, long ago. This scanning of her memory, upon command for these stories of her life, was somewhat like viewing a giant, faded montage of a thousand mental snapshots. Her mind's eye panned over the collage, and as she focused on one picture, it suddenly became larger than life, blossoming into glorious living color. The characters veritably jumped off the collage causing her heart to stir with a kind of longing — a longing for the past, for the way it truly was so long ago...

CHAPTER I

The hushed stillness of the forest was broken only by the sound of their footsteps crunching on the soft carpet of pine needles. It was early morning; Lisl and her father were out on one of their frequent hunts for the wild mushrooms that were native to their part of the country. The majestic Bavarian forests that surrounded their little village had always held a special fascination for young Lisl, and now as father and daughter trudged deeper into the woods, the child's legs stumbled to keep up with her father's long strides. Slanted shafts of sunlight pierced the canopy of pines and lent a magical touch to the air that fairly sparkled with the crispness of early May in Germany.

"Here are some, Father!" Lisl shouted excitedly as she ran to a large patch of fat mushrooms, their delicate aroma mingling with the pine.

"Mama will fix a wonderful soup for us tonight, Little One," Michael replied as he stooped to gather the cream-colored mushrooms for their basket.

The year was 1934. Lisl was six years old and the youngest of four children — all girls. With her flaxen blonde locks and large blue-green eyes, she was already showing promise of the beauty to come. Her parents were well into their forties when Lisl was born. For as long as she could remember, they had called her "Little One," more as an endearment than a reference to her size or age.

Her father Michael Wenzel was, for the most part, a quiet man. Totally unassuming, he was of medium height, bald, high cheek bones, a small neat mustache, and the palest blue eyes that seemed to twinkle constantly. A devoted family man, he worked hard every day, but never missed a chance to hug his children or tell a good joke.

Lisl adored both her parents, but she knew she was the apple of her father's eye. Right now, as she ran behind him in the woods, she wished he would walk slower so she could keep up.

"Can we pick strawberries, too, if we find them, Father?" Lisl asked.

Michael laughed as he took his daughter's hand, "It's not time for strawberries yet. We won't have those till later in the summer."

All too soon their hunt was over, for the large wicker basket her father had been carrying was brimming with the fragrant mushrooms they had come into the woods to find. As Michael strapped the basket to the back of the bicycle, Lisl noticed a few other people along the roadside apparently doing the same thing. "How does everybody know when to come out to look for mushrooms, Father?"

"Grown-ups know the seasons of different things like mushrooms and strawberries, and they teach these things to their children; then those children tell their children and so on. That's how it is through the ages, how people learn about farming, about housework, about raising children, about everything," Michael replied, leaning down to tweak her nose. "You learn it from your parents. Now, if you're through asking questions for a while, I suggest we get home. I'm sure Mama is preparing lunch by now. And I don't know about you, but I've worked up quite an appetite."

As she hopped onto her small bicycle, Lisl knew she was lucky. Lucky to have her wonderful father and mother. She knew other children at school who were not as fortunate. Why, her good friend, Trudi, had lost her father in a farming accident just last year. And there was that crippled boy who had come down from Dietfurt to live with his aunt here in Altmannstein. Indeed, Lisl realized, she was blessed with two loving parents and a sunny childhood, and in that particular year of 1934, German farm life, as the Wenzels knew it, was good. The problems of the big cities, rising unemployment and an economy teetering on the brink of disaster, were simply not felt as severely in rural Germany, certainly not for a six-year-old child wrapped up and sheltered in the warmth provided by loving parents. The impending war was light-years away, in another world so it seemed. No one knew even then what was in store for all, not only the horrors of war, the atrocities, the Holocaust, but the loss of innocence for everyone — young, old, East or West. Hitler had been installed as Chancellor the previous year; the German parliament or *Reichstag* had been dissolved, and the Nazi Party was well entrenched in the German government.

In the idyllic village of Altmannstein, however, life remained pure and unchanged by distant politics. In her warmly-cocooned world, the hunt for wild mushrooms was only one of countless adventures that filled young Lisl's days of growing up in Altmannstein.

Nestled in a valley and surrounded by Bavarian hills, the town of Altmannstein lies one hundred and six kilometers north of the city of Munich. It is a quaint little village whose very beginnings date back to the Middle Ages when the Holy Roman Empire extended its reach across Europe and beyond. Many of its original buildings are still standing, their architecture characterized by a pleasing combination of Byzantine-influenced onion-domed towers mixed with tall, angular Gothic church spires all untouched by time. Written documentation of the history of Altmannstein dates back all the way to the year 260 A.D. The town as it's known today, however, was developed more in the 12th Century. As is typical of any medieval town, all life surrounded the church. Altmannstein's Holy Cross Catholic Church, built in 1197, stands at the heart of the community. In 1331 Kaiser Ludwig I of Bavaria built an imposing fortress on a bluff overlooking the tiny village — imposing and ready to stand guard for its citizens. In 1633 the town and the castle were both devastated during the course of the Thirty-Year War. All that remained standing was a jagged-edged tower that, to this day, has become the famous landmark for the modern day Altmannstein.

Today, Altmannstein is well-known throughout the southern region of Bavaria as a pleasant holiday resort and spa complete with heated pools, tennis courts, a water park, and all the other amenities of a modern day vacation spot. Its very location places it at the heart of the "Romantic Route," a region of picturesque scenery and winding walkways ideal for Sunday strolls. Fortunately, today the area surrounding Altmannstein in all its rustic splendor has been designated as a national wildlife preserve maintained and protected by the state. So much of the breathtaking beauty of the hills and valleys of her homeland stayed with Lisl through the years, woven into the fiber of her being, as though the natural beauty of the land she had known as a child had actually become a part of her.

In 1934, first grade began in a five-story schoolhouse that was already three hundred years old at that time. Daily Mass was a way of life for the community and so the historic Holy Cross Catholic Church located across from the schoolhouse was where Lisl began her day. After Mass her daily ritual continued at the bakery where she bought her favorite sweet roll each morning before starting classes.

"*Danke, Herr* Steinberg," Lisl smiled as she reached over the counter to take the warm roll from the baker. Outside in the early morning sunshine, she settled down on the stone steps of the bakery to munch on the soft pastry. The warm, yeasty fragrance from the bakery wafted outside each time the door opened and closed from classmates buying their sweet rolls.

"Did you do your homework last night?" Rosa Weintraub asked as she plopped down next to Lisl. Being seated alphabetically in school, Rosa had always been placed next to Lisl ever since kindergarten as their last names both began with a "W." A child rather large for her age, Rosa towered over the others in the schoolyard. Most of the other girls were a little intimidated by Rosa, but it wasn't just her height that was intimidating. Rosa had a pugnacious demeanor; she was always harassing other children at playtime. However, Lisl suspected that the girl may have been just lonely and had developed her argumentative personality as a cover up, and so Lisl always managed to get along with her.

"Of course, I always do."

"Let me copy it from you again, one more time. I didn't have time to do mine last night," Rosa wheedled, casting a sidelong glance at Lisl.

"No, Rosa, I'm not going to let you copy my homework anymore. It's not fair. You should learn to do your own work," Lisl replied.

"Fine. I'll just find someone else, Miss Stuck-up," Rosa yelled over her shoulder as she ran toward the schoolhouse door, her fat, yellow pigtails bouncing heavily on her shoulders.

Lisl sighed. Sometimes there's just no getting along with people. Lisl didn't want to give her homework to Rosa to copy. Although she had allowed it a few times in the past, she knew it was wrong, and, if caught, both girls would be punished with a sharp rap across the knuckles from a stern yardstick-wielding teacher. But, more than that, she didn't want someone like Rosa to like her just for her homework. She wished Rosa could be a more sincere friend. She made a mental note to be extra nice to Rosa today even though she had refused Rosa's demands.

At lunch time the young Lisl always traded her home-baked bread for a classmate's bakery-made bread thinking, perhaps, it tasted better. As a farm child, she naturally assumed anything store-bought was always better. After school Lisl hurried home to help with the various chores that awaited her: helping her mother with the bread-baking and delivering fresh buttermilk in large vats to other women in the neighborhood.

Running up the road after classes were over, Lisl spotted her mother removing the fifteen or so loaves of bread from the hot brick oven that stood just outside their house. Maria, was a petite woman with classic features and whose face had already developed a fine web of laugh lines at the corners of her eyes by the time her fourth child came along. To the young Lisl, she was always the essence of maternal love as well as the epitome of the loving wife. Her mother was the one who, throughout their life, kept their home the warm, welcoming haven that Lisl remembered so well.

Her parents had married in 1909 in Pfaffenhofen, a large community north of Munich. Maria had been a master chef at a local restaurant there, and Michael had been the brew master for the local brewery that adjoined the restaurant. At twenty-one, Michael prided himself on being the youngest degreed brew master around. He had swept the young Maria off her feet, and together they shared a dream.

Dreams became reality and so, after the birth of their first daughter whom they named Maria, they escaped city life and purchased a farm in Altmannstein where they had three more children — all girls. Maria worked hard alongside Michael in the fields and, in spite of a life-long battle with asthma, never complained. She was there every day for all her girls: to bandage their wounds, to nurse them when they were ill, and to comfort them when they cried. Her three sisters were all much older than Lisl, and so, for most of her developing years, she was the only child in the household.

"You're just in time, Little One," Maria smiled at her youngest daughter, "the butter is ready, too."

Lisl dutifully put on her apron and helped her mother slide out the last of the fragrant loaves. "Mama, we had some strange visitors at school today," Lisl remarked as she dipped into the churn for a little butter.

Maria sliced deep into the crusty rye bread and sat down for a modest snack of bread and butter with her daughter. "What kind of visitors were they?"

"Men in uniforms — they came and told us to take down our picture of *Herr* Paul von Hindenburg," Lisl replied, her eyes wide with curiosity.

"How strange," Maria tried to keep the uneasiness from her voice.

"Why did they do that, Mama?"

"I don't know. Did your *Lehrer* say anything to them?"

"Yes, but we couldn't hear because *Herr* Kohler took the men out into the hallway right away. After the men left, *Herr* Kohler put *Herr* Hindenburg's picture right back up again. He was supposed to leave up a picture of that angry man with the little mustache, but he didn't. Do you think he'll get into trouble for that, Mama? Let's ask Father about it when he comes home tonight. Maybe he'll know what it was all about."

Maria frowned. There were so many disturbing reports in the papers these days. Political unrest, each party promising the same things, and, yet so much confusion, it was hard to tell who or what was best for the country. "Yes, your father can surely explain it to us, but I'm sure it's nothing to worry about. For right now, it's getting late and *Frau* Hohenstein and *Frau* Ziegler are waiting for their buttermilk, so you'll need to hurry."

Before her daughter left to deliver the buttermilk to the waiting neighbors, Maria placed a small lump of butter in the milk as a little gift. She knew that in these uncertain times seemingly insignificant things such as a small lump of butter in the buttermilk one bought were a delight to those who struggled each day to make ends meet.

Sunday was always Lisl's favorite day of the week. It was such a leisurely time for all of them. The family truly kept the Fourth Commandment: they kept holy the Sabbath and rested. Maria delighted in always dressing her youngest in white ruffled dresses topped off with a big floppy white bow in her hair. The active child always had trouble keeping the bow pinned securely even though her straight, fine hair was cut in the style of the day: short, blunt, and pixie-ish as if a bowl had been placed on her head and the hair cut around it.

After High Mass the family came home, and Maria cooked a wonderful feast of roasted chicken or goose, wilted cucumber salad, and boiled new potatoes. After the sumptuous meal, one could wander outside and, from the radio, hear the strains of a Strauss waltz drifting through the air as neighbors opened their windows to the warm sunshine. Finely starched white curtains billowed softly in the breeze, and the aroma of roast chicken wafted in the air.

Later in the evening the Wenzels always took the child *spatzieren*, a uniquely Bavarian habit in which neighbors strolled around the neighborhood to enjoy the cool evening air and admire each other's flower gardens. People practically competed with each other to see who could come up with the most riotous color, the largest snapdragons, the most brilliant gladioli. Each flower garden was cultivated right out front for the whole world to see. It was a genteel time in their little part of the world, one where people were courteous to each other and Sundays were meant for visiting and camaraderie with one's neighbors.

Growing up as the beloved youngest child of a middle-aged farm couple had its ups-and-downs, especially when it came to siblings. Many Sundays Lisl would find herself in the dubious care of her older sister, Anne, and her fiancé, Ludwig. The child would tag along as, hand-in-hand, they strolled the scenic countryside surrounding their town. Although the three of them explored the hills and vales of Altmannstein, the young Lisl was totally oblivious to the couple's yearning to be alone, and they, unfortunately, were totally oblivious to her. Each time that she pointed out to them an interesting work of nature — the brilliant red of a wild poppy's petals or a delicate spider's web sparkling with dew, she was met with distracted murmurs of "Fine, fine, Lisl," as the lovers gazed deep into each other's eyes.

How could these two people not share her enthusiasm for all the wondrous things in nature that surrounded them? she thought peevishly.

Running ahead of them up a hillside one warm Sunday afternoon, Lisl pointed to a craggy rock and yelled gleefully, "Let's stop here to rest. This is my very favorite look-out point in the whole world."

Anne and Ludwig, barely taking their eyes off each other, followed her to the boulder that to the girl's fanciful imagination resembled a roaring lion. The three of them climbed up onto the large rock and gazed out at the breathtaking vista that spread out before them. The gently rolling hills were covered with an intricate patchwork of freshly plowed fields checkered with brilliant green meadows. Dotting the landscape were pristine white houses, their windows underlined with planter boxes that spilled out in a riotous blaze of red geraniums. Stately birch trees lined the country roads that wound their way into the hazy distance. Above it all, billowy cotton puffs of clouds drifted lazily across a cerulean blue sky. A gentle breeze lifted a lock of her hair as Lisl perched contentedly on the sun-warmed rock and enjoyed the view.

After a few moments Ludwig turned brightly to Anne and said, "Anybody getting thirsty? I know I could use a lemonade."

"Oh, yes, that would be nice," Anne replied.

Ludwig reached in his pocket and handing the child some

coins said, "Lisl, will you run to the store, please, and get us three lemonades?"

"Okay, but only if you both wait here for me," she said.

"Of course, we'll wait right here," he replied with a smile as he reached out to ruffle her hair.

She skipped and ran all the way back into town to purchase their drinks. Clutching the three bottles of lemonade in her chubby hands, she hurried to climb back up the hill to where she had left Anne and Ludwig. When she reached the familiar boulder, she discovered to her dismay that they were nowhere in sight. Her sister and her boyfriend had abandoned her, and now she was alone! Tears welled up in the girl's eyes as she soon realized she had been duped. Those two had deliberately sent her on an errand so that they could be alone! Little did she know, at the time, that the delinquent two were hiding behind a grove of trees close by and were watching her all the while.

Still holding the lemonade bottles, Lisl cried as she ran back into town and up the street that led to her house. Soon she spotted her parents sitting on the garden bench in front of the house. Sobbing inconsolably, she ran to climb up on her mother's lap. Between hiccups Lisl told Maria and Michael the sad tale of how she had been abandoned by Anne and Ludwig. With a smile tugging at the corners of her lips, Maria soothed her daughter's hurt feelings by promising severe retribution against the offending sister. Michael turned his head to suppress the laughter that bubbled up inside as he thought of the young lovers escaping their baby-sitting duties for the rare chance to be alone. Gruffly he, too, promised a stern lecture for Anne and her fiancé. Feeling as though she had been avenged by her loving parents, Lisl dried her tears and ran off to play with friends down the street.

Although she had no way of knowing it at the time, Lisl realized much later in life how truly fortunate she had been as a child to be able to roam near and wide in the rural Altmannstein of the 1930s where violent crime was virtually nonexistent. Children played freely, not only in the streets of town, but were encouraged to explore the hills and valleys of the beautiful countryside.

Coming into a family as late in life as she did, there was very little sibling rivalry between Lisl and her sisters. The oldest, Maria had already married and left home when Lisl was four, and the other two, Anne and Frieda, were getting married within months of each other. With July approaching, Anne announced her engagement and Lisl was honored to be chosen as the flower girl in her wedding. For weeks the Wenzel household bustled with preparations for the big event. There was food to be cooked, flowers to arrange, and, of course, dresses to sew.

Wide-eyed with wonder, the young Lisl gazed in fascination at the clouds of gossamer tulle used for the bride's veil that would trail endlessly behind her. At each fitting, the attending women ooh'ed and aah'ed at the way the shimmering satin wedding dress draped and hugged the entire length of Anne's slim figure. When the big day finally came, Lisl solemnly walked toward the altar in slow step with the music, then turned to watch her sister float down the aisle on their father's arm. Lisl was convinced that Anne was lovelier than any storybook princess. Her white satin lace gown was high-necked with narrow fitted sleeves. The skirt was draped and gathered in a pouf of a train that trailed regally behind her. On her head a simple garland of white roses and sprigs of green asparagus fern held the delicate veil of tulle in place. She carried more white roses and green asparagus fern over her left arm. The church was filled to overflowing with all the family, friends and neighbors that turned out for the festive occasion.

Once the ceremony was over, the townspeople followed the bridal couple as they walked down the street to the nearby restaurant, a gasthaus, for the reception dinner followed by a dance. The food was always abundant — no guest walked away hungry. The tables fairly groaned with the weight of the immense platters of huge hams, roasts, cold cuts, and potatoes, trays of relish, and an endless variety of cakes and *torten*, that uniquely rich multi-layered confection that has evolved through the centuries into practically an art form throughout Germany and Austria.

At the dance the real fun began, for an age-old custom of the times was the stealing of the bride by members of the wedding party at some point during the reception. Unbeknownst to the groom, the bride would be whisked away to an undisclosed location. Then, the object of the game was for the groom to find her. He had to find her rather quickly, for while he was searching high and low for his new bride, the kidnapping party was eating and drinking up a tab for which the groom was ultimately responsible. The food, music and laughter lasted well into the night. Reluctantly, Lisl, the little flower girl, was taken home by a neighbor at ten p.m. when it was time for her to go to bed. Fighting the fatigue that washed over her, she climbed into bed and dreamed of the day when she, too, would have such a grand wedding.

All the talk and excitement of Anne's wedding had barely died down when the planning activities started all over again for Frieda's nuptials. Once again the house buzzed with activity. Michael Wenzel moaned dramatically that two weddings so close together would wipe him out financially, but secretly he was pleased that two more of his daughters had found happiness with good husbands.

Soon Lisl found herself the only child in the household — no longer taunted by older sisters, yet given to a sense of loneliness as a result of the loss of her siblings.

Michael, in an attempt to assuage her feelings of loneliness, decided one day to take Lisl to an auction. Once a year at this time, the county held the auction to sell off, among other things, some of the many cherry trees that lined the roads leading out of town.

Hand-in-hand, Michael and Lisl walked down to the marktplatz at the center of town, where people were already milling about. The men, mostly local merchants, stood in groups puffing their pipes and comparing stories of their most recent business deals to see who had the most business prowess and acumen. Here and there children darted in and out of the crowds. A few women in well-tailored suits stood on the sidelines waiting for the auction to begin. It was early morning and quite cool for August. The sun had just risen over the hill, splaying its golden rays in a dramatic semicircle around the jagged stone tower that overlooked Altmannstein. A makeshift stage was set up on one end of the central courtyard that served as a marketplace, and the auctioneer was already at his place at the podium looking over the list of items.

Lisl and her father headed for a small table at the side and picked up a copy of the list.

"Now, Little One," Michael instructed, "you must behave yourself when the auction begins because if you raise your arm for any reason, we may find ourselves buying something we don't want."

"Will we buy anything at all, Father?" the child asked.

"Perhaps."

"If I had the money, I know what I'd want."

"And what might that be, if you had the money?"

"I want one of those wonderful cherry trees growing along the road that goes out to the Altmühl!" Lisl exclaimed. Lisl loved the famous little stream that twisted and wound through the outskirts of town as it made its way to the Danube. She had spent many languid summer afternoons exploring the cool and shady banks of the Altmühl after munching handfuls of cherries from the trees lining the road that led to the picturesque "old mill" stream.

"A cherry tree, huh?" Michael eyed her skeptically. "And what would you do with a cherry tree if you owned one?"

"Why, I'd climb up into it every day and eat all the cherries so that the branches wouldn't be weighed down with all that fruit. And then it could grow even taller!"

Michael roared with laughter at the child's logic. "Then let's see if we can buy you a tree."

With a sudden pounding of the gavel, the auctioneer began. To Lisl it was a confusion of sounds and gestures. Everything was happening quickly. It was as if the auctioneer spoke a totally different language and only a privileged few in the audience could understand him. Suddenly, Lisl heard two words she could understand: "cherry tree." She looked up to see her father give an almost imperceivable nod. The auctioneer at the podium pointed his gavel to her father and continued his rapid-fire monologue. Someone else in the crowd held up a small sign and the auctioneer immediately pointed to that person. Michael nodded again and once more the gavel was pointed back at him. Lisl watched in fascination as back and forth the stranger and her father competed for the same tree. Finally, as the bidding slowed, the gavel still pointing in the stranger's direction, Lisl, in a moment of panic and confusion, raised her hand. The auctioneer slammed the gavel down, cheers rose from the crowd, and a stunned Lisl was looking up into the stern, unsmiling eyes of her father.

"Young lady, is seems you have just bought us a cherry tree."

"I didn't know what to do, Father," she cried. "It looked like that man was going to get our tree, and I just couldn't let him do that! I'm sorry, Father, can we afford it? Will I be punished for this?"

"No, Lisl," Michael said with a resigned sigh, " I just wish you had waited. There were other trees to bid on, my dear."

Lisl felt deep remorse for displeasing her father. Yet something inside her cried out with joy that now she owned her very own cherry tree!

The next day after school she raced home to change from her school uniform to her play clothes and join her waiting friends, Trudi, Max and Berta, who were already waiting for her on the road. Laughing and shouting, the four of them climbed up into the huge tree at once and began eating the luscious ripe fruit.

Once satiated from all the cherries, Lisl realized with alarm that she was hopelessly late for supper. The friends quickly parted company, and Lisl hurried home to find the family already seated at the table eating dinner.

Maria shot her an admonishing look over her bifocals as the girl tried to explain her tardiness. "Mama, I'm sorry I'm late — we had such fun in the cherry tree and I lost all track of time!" she explained, her little hands turned up in a helpless shrug.

Michael's chair screeched as he got up to stand beside her and said, "That's alright this time, Little One. Now say the dinner prayer alone for us."

Everyone stood up and faced the crucifix on the wall. Lisl wide-eyed with fear had never said the dinner prayer alone and was now embarrassed and humiliated at being singled out like this. The child choked back her tears and stammered the prayer the best she could, vowing never to be late again!

CHAPTER 2

Having recovered from the personal financial blow of two weddings in one year, Michael Wenzel looked forward to the future with hopes of a better new year, 1935. Alas, it was not to be. Germany suffered greater economic woes than ever before with all national resources being allocated to the massive, grand-scale rearmament of the country. The Wenzels continued to go about their lives as normally as possible even thought the quality of living had become noticeably shabbier in a national sacrifice for the build-up of a mighty military. In spite of the country's ills, winter melted into spring, spring warmed to summer, and in July of 1937, Lisl was faced with the prospect of an exciting trip to Munich to visit her oldest sister Maria. As Lisl grew older, these visits to Munich were to become a treasured annual adventure.

"What's *München* like, Father?" Lisl asked as she leaned forward to watch the rolling hills and meadows float past them outside the window as the train clickity-clacked through the countryside. The picturesque landscape was ever-changing as dark patches of forest gave way to emerald green vales. Tucked at the bottom of these vales occasionally were clusters of houses that marked another one of countless villages. At the center of each cluster of buildings was the inevitable white church spire that towered above the other buildings and pierced the cobalt sky.

Michael leaned back clasping his hands behind his head. "Ah, *München*! *München* is nothing like Altmannstein. To us, it is one of the greatest cities in the world. It is truly a European center of art.

Maria will take you to fine museums, to symphony concerts, perhaps to an opera. There's even a grand old castle you can visit," he said gazing out the window. "It will be a wonderful time for you."

Lisl's favorite subjects in school, now that she was in the fourth grade, were art and music, and the thought of actually going to an opera or an historic castle was beyond her wildest expectations!

"Yoo-hoo, Lisl! Father!" Maria stood on the platform waving to the pair stepping down from the train as it rolled into the station.

"Maria!" Lisl hailed her eldest sister as she ran ahead of her father to give Maria an affectionate hug. "It's so good to see you!"

"I hope you can stay a while. I have all kinds of wonderful things planned for us to do," Maria said excitedly as she helped Lisl with her bags. After bidding their father farewell and seeing him off on the return train to Altmannstein, the two sisters linked arms and walked to the waiting car. Rather than take the trolley, Maria had hired a car in which to bring Lisl home to her apartment. Franz, her husband, was to be out-of-town on banking business so the two sisters had the entire week to themselves. As the car rolled past the tall wrought iron gates and into the gravel driveway, Lisl gazed in wonder at the elegant townhouse apartment before her. The driver carried her bags in behind her, then discreetly disappeared while Lisl followed her sister into the vast hallway. Their heels clicked on the cool marble floor as the hallway opened up to a spacious living room.

Maria shunned the popular taste in furnishings of the times — the heavy, ornate furniture and dark rooms so prized by her elite friends. Instead, she preferred the clean lines and light blond oaks of a more contemporary look. Lisl's eyes widened with pleasure at the tastefully appointed rooms — settees covered in chinz and tiny coffee tables surrounded by palms and frothy ferns. A plain but graceful china cabinet stood against the far wall, its crystal and porcelain contents gleaming through leaded glass double doors. Lisl unpacked her bags in her room and then joined her sister for coffee and fresh *pflaumenkuchen* in the breakfast room. Lisl delighted in the delicate feel of the paper-thin Meissen cup in her hands as she sipped the weak coffee which had been laced heavily with warm milk.

Maria's wealth was apparent but not conspicuous. Understated elegance, Lisl thought. Her sister did not clutter her home with the knick knacks and baubles that were the fashion, but the few items she did display were of the absolute highest quality. Her only concession to being fashionably showy was the Bechstein piano that stood regally in the corner of the drawing room. What a magnificent work it was, thought Lisl, as she ran her hands over the polished mahogany surface. Someday, she would have one. If she could convince Father to buy her one, that is. And, of course, there would be lessons — that could be expensive. She wasn't sure if her parents would be able to afford it all. But, oh, how her fingers ached to fly over the ivory keys playing beautiful rhapsodies, sonatas and concertos that would joyously fill the house with music. Yes, she would definitely remember to ask Father when he came to fetch her the following Sunday if she could have a piano.

Maria thoroughly enjoyed showing Lisl the sights of Munich, and Lisl, her eyes shining, drank in the culture with all her senses. Lisl discovered that she had a passion for the hustle and bustle of urban life as the two spent hours walking around the crowded city. The new *Führer* and *Reichskanzler*, Adolph Hitler, had recently reinstated conscription so everywhere you looked there were posters calling men to arms to serve their homeland. Every now and then, Lisl and Maria passed a band of marching Brownshirts or a small group of them passing out fliers on the street corner. Each time Lisl would look curiously at these strange young men with the steely look in their eyes.

"Don't stare at them. They have been known to be violent on occasion." Maria took her sister's arm and hurried her down the street.

They spent long, leisurely afternoons at the museums; they picnicked by the side of the lake in the park; they thrilled to the swelling strains of a Schubert symphony. One particularly beautiful morning, the two sisters rode bicycles to the park in the center of the city. Maria rented a boat so they could row leisurely across the pond.

"Have you ever rowed a boat before, Lisl?" Maria asked.

"No, but it doesn't look that difficult," Lisl replied surveying the small vessel.

"Watch your step. That's it, easy now," Maria guided her youngest sister as she stepped gingerly into the swaying boat. "Now, just pick up that oar and paddle like this."

Soon the two of them were rowing the craft smoothly across the water, their silver ripples breaking the glassy surface of the pond. Several large swans, one of them jet black, swam gracefully around them. As Lisl and Maria let go of the oars and began drifting lazily in the sunshine, Lisl held out her hand to the black swan which promptly nipped her fingers.

"Ow! Did you see what he did? That's a mean one! I thought swans were supposed to be gentle and shy. They look so graceful when they swim," Lisl remarked as she examined her finger for any serious injury.

"He just thought you were holding out food to him," Maria laughed. "People around here feed these birds all the time. That's why they're so fat and sleek. I guess that will teach you a lesson not to stick your hand out to strange swans!"

Lisl leaned back to enjoy the sunshine, and Maria studied her little sister with an amused smile. "What do you want to be when you grow up, Lisl?"

Lisl spotted three monks sitting on a park bench on the banks of the pond. Their bald heads were bent together as the three were engrossed in thoughtful conversation. Their brown robes tied with ropes at the waist and the simple sandals on their feet provided stark contrast to the fashion finery of the city people strolling by.

Lisl's brows knitted together seriously. "Well, I've given it a lot of thought, and I've decided to become a nun. I feel that I have the calling."

Maria's eyes flew open in surprise. "No! Not a nun! You can't. Why, you simply can't. Whatever possessed you to think you would ever want to be a nun?" Maria's hands flew up in the air making the boat rock dangerously off balance.

"Why not?" Lisl tried to look indignant. "It's my life and I can be a nun if I want to, can't I? I mean, there's nothing wrong with that, is there?"

"Well, of course, there's nothing wrong with it. We're a religious family all right. It's just that. . ." Maria felt she had to frame her words carefully if Lisl were actually contemplating a cloistered life. "It's just that you're so bright, so full of life, it would seem like almost a waste if you couldn't have a full life with a husband and children. . . and. . . and. . . oh, I don't know, Lisl! Don't become a nun!" Maria almost pleaded with her sister.

Lisl could no longer maintain the serious face and burst out laughing at the sight of her sister stammering and sputtering. "I'm teasing you!" she cried with a triumphant smile.

"Why, you little trickster! You really had me going for a minute," Maria scolded letting her hand drop in the water to flick a small splash of water at Lisl in retaliation.

Lisl returned the spray and soon both sisters were hurling rapid handfuls of water at each other, the droplets sparkling in the sun. Inevitably the boat overturned in the pond, and the two found themselves shrieking and laughing while trying to tread water. Their clothing ballooned in the water around them.

"Have you had enough, you little monster?" Maria laughed between gulps.

Wild-eyed with terror, Lisl suddenly realized the water was deeper than she had thought and cried out as she thrashed about trying to keep her head above the water, "Maria, I can't swim!"

Maria saw that this was no joke and quickly swam to her sister's side, placing her hand under Lisl's stomach for support. "Move your arms like this. There you go — just like that. Hold your head up and move the water away from you. Don't forget to kick." Within minutes Maria had Lisl doing a fairly competent breast stroke. Fortunately, the water was only shoulder-deep for Maria who quickly guided her sister safely to the banks.

"Now look what we've done. We're soaking wet; what will people think?" Lisl giggled as she wrung out the hem of her skirt.

"It's almost dark. Let's go home and get into some dry clothes. We'll need to get some rest as we'll start early tomorrow. We're taking the train to see the famous Schloss Neuschwanstein — it's truly beautiful this time of year! Wait till you see it!"

The fairy tale castle was everything Maria promised and more. Neuschwanstein was one of the three famous castles built by King

Ludwig II of Bavaria in the nineteenth century. "King Ludwig I's grandson King Ludwig II was actually born in *München,* but he lived his last years here in this castle. He was tragically out of touch with his era. They say he was mad, you know, King Ludwig II, because he loved the Middle Ages and built these castles to reflect that era," Maria remarked as they walked through the Gateway Tower into the vast Entrance Hall. High vaulted ceilings, giant statuary, and walls adorned with intricately painted friezes of hunting scenes were everywhere. In the Octagonal Tower Lisl gazed up at the towering marble statue of St. George.

Maria took her arm and led her up the winding staircase to the king's living quarters. "King Ludwig II had a romantic wish to revive medieval knighthood," she said. The sumptuous bedroom was dark and Gothic with red silk curtains, and benches with leather cushions richly tooled with the coats of arms of Wittelsbach, Schwangau and Bavaria. "Look out that portal. You can see the Alpsee from here."

Lisl was overwhelmed by the grandeur of it all. "Oh, Maria, wouldn't it be absolutely wonderful to live here. I could be a fairy princess, and Mama and Father could be the queen and king of Bavaria!" she exclaimed, her eyes shining brightly.

"Don't get too carried away, Little Sister. You'd be lonely and bored way up here on this mountain top. We don't want you to go mad like King Ludwig," Maria laughed. "It's all very medieval. Looking around at all this splendor I think King Ludwig II was, perhaps, just a man who didn't fit his time. He lived in the eighteen hundreds and left these three castles, Neuschwanstein, Linderhof and Herrenchiemsee as his legacy."

"What happened to him?" Lisl asked as they continued their tour.

"Well, the exact circumstances of his death were never known. Toward the end of his life, he was living under house arrest because he was considered incurably delusional; and one night in June of 1886, he drowned in the dark waters of the Starnbergersee."

Lisl tried to imagine the tragic young king as he lived his lonely life in this dark and looming castle. The two sisters wandered from room to room, each more opulent than the last. Lisl marveled at the inlaid gold everywhere, the gilt ceilings, the decorative frescoes, the vast mirrored halls that rivaled Versailles.

"I don't think I've ever seen anything more beautiful!" Lisl exclaimed. Her face was turned up to gaze in awe at the glittering surroundings.

Outside in the brilliant sunlight, they started on the twenty-minute walk down the mountain to Hohenschwangau, the castle directly behind Neuschwanstein. This lesser-known but equally-opulent palace built by King Ludwig II's father, Maximilian II was where the young Ludwig II spent his childhood. Once there, Lisl and Maria strolled through the impeccably manicured rose gardens that graced Hohenschwangau. Lisl looked around at the virtual sea of pinks, reds, lavenders and peach flowers bordered by tightly clipped boxwood hedges and interspersed with a maze of gravel walkways. Roses of every variety bloomed in outrageous bursts of color and fragrance in these formal gardens. Just walking through them in the palatial atmosphere made Lisl feel like royalty.

The following Sunday morning, Lisl realized that the week in Munich had flown by for her, and all too soon her visit with Maria was drawing to an end. With her bags already packed, Lisl stood in the courtyard outside the apartment's front door and listened as hundreds of church bells all over the city rang out at one time, their sweet clamor calling the faithful to Mass. Lisl was dressed and ready to go to Mass before her father was scheduled to come at one-o'clock to pick her up and take her back home.

"Today we're going to Mass at the Marienkirche, one of the most beautiful cathedrals in Munich," Maria called out to her from the hallway.

Lisl looked down at her skirt. "Am I dressed up enough for such a fine cathedral? She was clad in the new white organdy blouse Maria had bought her and her one good skirt, navy blue with accordion pleats.

Maria looked at her sibling, her eyes brimming with pride.

"You look quite chic, my little sister. Let me just get my key and we'll be off."

The Mass was more moving and meaningful than any sightseeing

Lisl had done during the past week. The famous cathedral was filled with people, their every movement echoing in the vast chamber. Lisl's eyes followed the curling incense smoke as it spiraled upward to touch the winged cherubs in every corner of the cavernous ceiling. As the priest chanted, a heavenly choir of children's voices rose from the choir loft and swelled in a hymn of praise so pure, so sweet, it brought tears to Lisl's eyes as it rang out and echoed in the hallowed cathedral.

"Take care of yourself, Lisl," Maria smiled. "And you, too, Father." The three were standing once again on the train platform as Lisl and Michael prepared for their trip back to Altmannstein.

"This has been a trip I will never forget!" Lisl called over her shoulder as she stepped onto the train.

Maria stood on the platform and waved to them until the train was completely out of sight.

As autumn neared, the Wenzels prepared for an abundant harvest. Once the wheat had been gleaned, the hay baled and stored for winter, and the crops harvested, Michael performed the time-honored ritual of butchering a hog to sustain his family through the long, cold winter. Not only was the butchering a festive, family event where everyone pitched in with the work, but every part of the animal was put to practical use. The meat was cured; sausages were stuffed and smoked; the fat was rendered into lard; and even the feet were scrubbed and pickled. People who lived off the land learned to live efficiently with little waste or live without. As the weather turned colder, Michael took the slowly smoked meats from the smokehouse, and soon the whole family feasted on pork sausage, potato salad, and thick slabs of fresh bread slathered with butter.

Lisl relished the traditions of autumn. She awoke early one Saturday morning in October knowing that that day would be special. It seemed hard to believe that it was already fall. The summer had simply flown by; the harvesting was done, and in school they were already well into the semester. The six-weeks' summer vacation from school never seemed long enough. There was always so much to do. Today would be special, nevertheless. Resl Kornfeld was paying the family her annual visit to sew their clothes for Christmas.

Preparations for the holidays always began months in advance. As a small child Lisl always knew that the holidays were coming when her mother brought out the mail order catalog and ordered fabric for not only the family's wardrobe, but for household goods as well. Lisl ran her hands over the smooth damask her mother had ordered for their featherbed covers and the fine, pinpoint cotton needed for her father's tailored shirts. Bolts and bolts of fabric ready to be transformed into dresses, dish towels and nightgowns would arrive by mail.

Resl Kornfeld, the family's seamstress, was a handsome, middle-aged woman who came to the house eight weeks before Christmas. Lisl eagerly looked forward to her visits because, to the youngster, Resl was incredibly fascinating.

"Is she here? Is she here yet?" Lisl asked excitedly as she burst into the kitchen where her mother was taking hot rolls out of the oven.

"No — no, not yet," Maria answered patiently. "Please eat your breakfast, then go outside to play. She'll be along shortly."

Later that morning as she sat on the steps of the garden, Lisl spied the tall, primly dressed figure marching up the street towards the house.

"Resl! I'm so glad you've come," the child cried gaily as she ran up to greet her.

"It's good to see you, too, Lisl," she said. "Here, help me with my bags, will you?"

The girl matched her steps to the smiling woman's as they strode up to the house together.

"I can hardly wait to hear you tell your stories again," Lisl said.

Resl laughed, "You've heard them all before so many times!"

"I don't care," she replied, "to me, they're so interesting."

"Grüss *Gott, Frau* Wenzel. How have you been?" Resl greeted Maria breathlessly as she removed her hat and placed it on the table in the hall.

"Resl! It's always a pleasure to see you," Maria replied warmly. "I have some beautiful material for you this year — and my older daughters need some things made as well."

"Then let's get started," Resl said warming her hands over the stove.

Always gracious and impeccably dressed, Resl was a master storyteller. At tea time each afternoon, Maria brought out the honey-sweetened gingerbread cookies that she baked especially for the holidays, and Resl regaled them with never-ending stories of her childhood. Lisl sat enraptured by her magical weaving of tales from another era.

The living area of the Wenzel home was made up of the dining room and living room and served as the center of family activity. The room was dominated by a wood-burning stove, a large, comfortable couch and two chairs. White lace cafe curtains graced the windows. A long, scrubbed wooden table sat at one end of the room and the stove occupied the other. As the silent snow flakes of an early winter storm fell in the growing darkness outside, the room was warm and cozy with the heat that radiated from the glazed tiles of the wood-burning stove, and the fire cast a roseate glow about the room. On one end of the couch sat Maria knitting Michael's traditional Christmas socks, her bifocals perched on the end of her nose, and Lisl sat curled up at the other end asking one question after another, her blue-green eyes shining with anticipation. Resl, sitting in a straight-backed chair, sipped her tea and spun her stories. The only sounds were the steady ticking of the cuckoo clock on the wall joined occasionally by the intermittent crackle of the burning logs that hissed and popped softly in the stove.

Resl had grown up in the Nareiskaya district of Warsaw, one of the many Jewish neighborhoods that dotted the Polish capital. Her stories were always steeped in the habits and traditions of Jewish life in turn-of-the-century Poland.

She told of the solemn family tradition of lighting the menorah at Chanukah, and described the mouthwatering dishes her mother would make for the family: the herring, potato latkes, gefilte fish, and luscious fig tarts. Her world was one of no movie theaters, no cars, no streetlights, no billboards, no modern conveniences whatsoever. Horse-drawn wagons filled the cobblestone streets, and at every corner vendors hawked fresh fruits, vegetables, clothing, and tinned food from their pushcarts. Children ran and played games in the streets. Women in flower-print dresses hung out of windows to gossip. Nareiskaya's only link with the twentieth century was the trolley that ran through the center of the district.

Lisl was fascinated with the woman's description of her childhood classmates, particularly the boys so mysterious to her in their skullcaps and ear curls studying at the feet of their teachers — bearded men in dark blouses, breeches, and heavy boots. Resl had left that world long ago to settle in Bavaria. It was there that she earned a highly acclaimed reputation as a master seamstress.

It was apparent that Resl was fond of children, and so, it struck young Lisl as odd that for as long as she had known her, Resl never married. Her brother and sister also had moved to different parts of Europe, and her parents had apparently passed away when Resl was just a child. How sad, thought Lisl, that someone so lovely and sweet would choose to spend her life alone.

"Tell us another story, Resl," Lisl asked, "you never tell us much about your parents. What happened to them; how did you lose them?"

"Lisl!" Maria said sharply, "it isn't polite to ask about such personal things."

Resl's eyes clouded over darkly for a moment. Then as she regained her composure said," It's all right, *Frau* Wenzel. The child is just curious. I'll be glad to tell you, but I warn you, it's not a very pleasant story. I was about your age, Lisl. My parents had been working in the fields all day and had just come back to the house at dark, totally exhausted. I was in charge of watching my younger brother and sister while they had been gone. Later that night as we prepared for bed, we heard the thunder of hoof beats on the cobblestone streets outside. My mother told me to take my brother and sister and go hide in the hayloft of the barn. I did what I was told, for although I was confused and didn't know what was happening, I never questioned my mother."

Lisl sat hugging a sofa pillow and asked in a low voice, "Who was coming that was so dangerous that you had to hide from them?"

Resl smiled as she reached out to stroke the child's hair. "The soldiers on horseback that were galloping into our village were White Russians — Cossacks — who regularly raided Jewish neighborhoods like ours to burn and destroy houses and murder people in their beds."

Eyes wide with terror, Lisl whispered, "Why?"

"Throughout centuries, my people have always met with religious intolerance and the Cossacks were intent on wiping out Jews with these horrible pogroms. That night they set fire to the houses on our street including ours. I ran in my nightgown to the hayloft. I was carrying my baby sister and pulling my little brother by his arm. We hid under the straw in hopes that they would leave the barn alone. Fortunately, for some unknown reason, they did. During the night I heard shots ring out. The Cossacks were slaughtering men, women, children, dogs, livestock — anything that got in their way. People were crying and moaning everywhere. I tried to cover my ears to shut out the terrible noise. I heard my parents crying out in the burning house. I'll never forget the sound of my mother's screams. Both of them died that night. I stayed in the hayloft until the next morning when a surviving neighbor found us. After that, my sister and brother were sent to live with a relative, and I lived with the neighbor helping her with housework and sewing until I could leave the village on my own."

With tears in her eyes, Maria asked gently, "Did you ever find out what happened to your siblings?"

"No," Resl replied simply, "but I understand they are living in Austria right now, and I hope someday I can find them."

"Resl, we're so sorry you had to lose your parents in such a terrible way. You must know you will always be welcome in our home," Maria said.

"Thank you, *Frau* Wenzel, it... it was a long time ago, and I have made peace with my past," she smiled gently at them. "I'm afraid that what is happening in this country may be even worse. So many of my Jewish friends, especially in München and Ingolstadt, are not allowed to prosper and must hand over more and more of their earnings than ever before to the Reich."

"That's dreadful!" Maria exclaimed. "We, too, have to pay heavy farm taxes to the government, and yet the only things we read about in the newspapers are how the Reich is creating more jobs for the unemployed, and how Hitler has restored order out of chaos, and how he is taking a hard-line stand against the Communists that have threatened to take over our country for many years."

"I fear it will get worse for all of us before it gets any better," replied Resl darkly.

All too soon their visit was over, and it was time for Resl to get back to her sewing. Her petticoats rustled under her wool skirts as she walked across the polished, hardwood floor. Resl was an extremely talented seamstress who could work magic with a length of cloth. Within the course of a week, her fingers flew over the rich fabric. With just a nip here and a tuck there, she transformed the lengths of material into expertly tailored clothes including school dresses for Lisl, night wear for the whole family, and crisp, new shirts for Michael. The bolts of damask were used to make new covers for the family's down-filled featherbeds. Yards and yards of striped, cotton muslin soon became stacks of dish towels. Even the newly-wed older sisters, Anne and Frieda, received dozens of tea towels that Resl sewed for their household needs.

As Christmas drew nearer, Lisl accompanied her father into the woods to check their stand of beech trees. It was the custom of the times that at Christmas, families hiked out into the forests to select and cut down their own Christmas tree. Michael had his own copse of trees, and he wanted to make sure no one had taken any of theirs. Lisl waited impatiently while Maria bundled her up in what seemed like endless layers of clothing.

"Don't go without me, Father" she anxiously called out to him.

"I'll wait, don't worry," he replied.

She cheerfully ran alongside him as they trudged through the snow. The forest in winter was a magical wonderland for the young Lisl. With drifts as high as two feet, the snow glittered in the morning sun in an endless blanket of white diamonds. The majestic beech and spruce trees seemed to balance soft pillows of snow on their boughs, and the air held a tranquil quality. Every now and then the child would run ahead, select a smooth patch of snow, fall backwards on it and swing her arms wide in a joyful attempt at making the most magnificent snow angel ever.

"Look at this one, Father!" she exclaimed, "bet you can't do that!"

Her father would cast mildly disapproving glances in her direction as he made his way deeper into the woods. Michael took great pains to teach his daughter, from an early age, not only right from wrong, but how to exercise caution and develop a sense of direction when venturing out into unfamiliar territory.

Finally after the third or fourth angel, Michael helped his youngest up out of the snow, and, with a mischievous grin, said, "All right, watch this."

He unceremoniously plopped down on an undisturbed patch and flapped his arms like some giant bird trapped in the snow, while Lisl giggled at the sight of her dignified father making snow angels with her. They dusted the snow off themselves and turned around to inspect their artwork.

"Your angel has fatter wings than mine," Lisl observed with all the wisdom of her seven years.

"And yours, Little One, looks more like a real angel," her father smiled.

As the two continued into the woods, the child would shout out just to hear the crisp echo of her young voice reverberating in the forest that seemed to go on forever. Each time that she'd yell, she would run a little farther away from her father. Finally, as she listened to her echo fading away, she turned to run back to Michael. Suddenly, he was nowhere in sight. Her stomach lurched as she now realized she was lost. How could she have gone so far? In a panic, she ran in one direction, stopped, and shouted, "Father!"

The only answer was her own echo mocking her in her panic. Her heart pounding, she ran in another direction, stopped and called out again, "Father! Where are you?"

At that moment Michael stood up from behind a clump of bushes where he had been hiding and quietly said, "Here I am, Lisl. Let this be a lesson to you," he said, shaking his finger at her sternly, "never wander off in the forest by yourself again."

With relief the girl ran to him and threw her arms tightly around his waist.

"Never, Father?" she asked looking up at him.

"Well, at least not until you're old enough to know where you're going," he replied.

"I'll never wander away from you again no matter how old I am," she vowed resolutely.

"No, Little One, someday when you're grown, you'll meet a wonderful man, and you'll have to go wherever he goes."

"You mean when I marry?"

"Yes, when you marry." Michael imagined his youngest daughter grown up and married. He knew that when that day came, his heart would be broken forever. She meant so much to him, this golden child, and he wanted to protect her and shelter her from harm for always. His heart flooded with these emotions, yet his mind told him that it was inevitable that some day he would have to let her go.

"I won't want a man as long as I have you, Father," Lisl said looking up at him with a happy smile.

"You're still a little girl right now," he reproved gently. "When you're grown up, you must marry a good man who'll take care of you. I'll be too old by then."

Father and daughter walked along in silence as Lisl tried to imagine life with someone other than her father.

"Well, I'll just make sure we don't wander too far from you, Father." she stated matter-of-factly. "I'll always be here to take care of you when you get old, no matter what kind of man I marry. You have my promise!"

Michael smiled, stroked his daughter's head and mused, if only that were true. He already knew that at her early age, Lisl was special. As much as he loved his other three daughters, he knew in his heart of hearts that this one was the most precious. All fathers have a favorite child, he rationalized, the trick was not to let on to the others. He hoped that in rearing his older children, he had been as even-handed as possible. But, coming to Maria and him so late in life, Lisl was a rare gift that he could enjoy for a very short time. Something told him that she was meant for a greater destiny than Altmannstein could hold for her, and he dreaded the day when he would have to let her go. But, like a rare bird, she was meant to fly. Finally he said, "Let's get back home. Mama has some hot *Glühwein* waiting for us."

Soon the holy season was upon them, and the town dressed up in its finest. Swags of long-needled pine boughs draped over the doorway of every establishment in the *marktplatz*. Glittering snow blanketed the countryside. As Lisl sat in her room brushing her hair on the afternoon of Christmas Eve, she waited for her mother to call her downstairs and send her to Anne's house. Although it was 1937, in the wake of the Great Depression and no one had any money to speak of; yet, as a nine-year old child, Lisl never felt deprived. On the contrary, the child felt blessed with the wealth of tradition and the family warmth that surrounded her at the time.

She knew the Christmas tradition by heart: her mother and father would send her to her sister's house, a short walk away. The two of them would then bring the fresh, green beech tree into the living room and start decorating it with candles, bubble lights, and incredibly fragile, paper-thin glass ornaments. By the time she returned, the tree would be there to surprise her in all its sparkling splendor. Presents were always opened on Christmas Eve because that was when the Christ Child, or C*hristkindl*, came. The whole evening was such a magical and exciting time for children all over Germany — to celebrate the birth of Christ with family and friends on the Holy Night itself. Although the tradition seldom varied year after year, it never failed to capture Lisl's imagination as it captured millions of children's imaginations through the ages.

"Lisl, are you ready to go to Anne's?" her mother's voice drifted up to the girl's room.

"Yes, I'm coming!" Lisl answered bounding down the stairs in excitement.

"Now be sure to come home in time for dinner," her mother said as she buttoned the child's coat and pressed a kiss on her forehead.

"I won't be late," she promised.

The afternoon seemed to drag on endlessly as she visited with Anne and Ludwig. Her brother-in-law attempted to keep her entertained with card tricks, but her thoughts kept wandering to the wonderful Christmas tree that she knew her parents were decorating right now. Finally, Anne and Ludwig donned their coats from the hall closet, and the three of them started the short walk back to the Wenzel's house.

"Hurry, you two," Lisl said sliding down the icy path and narrow alleyways that led back to her parents' house.

Running ahead of Anne and Ludwig, she flung open the front door and stood in awe of the magnificent tree that had been placed near the window.

"Oh, Mama, Father! It's beautiful!" she cried as she clapped her hands in delight.

The four-foot beech tree was festooned with twinkling sparklers, glass birds with long, silky tails, ornate tear-drop shaped ornaments and was topped off with a shining, gold star. At the base of the tree lay a small mound of hand-decorated packages.

One of the other sisters, Frieda, and her husband Alfons were already seated in the living room, and Maria brought giant platters of sliced meats, cheeses, and bread to the table.

"Sure smells good," Ludwig said as he hugged the older woman.

Everyone talked and laughed as they gathered around the dining room table to enjoy the holiday repast. Part of the tradition of the holiday meal was a special treat that everyone enjoyed during those cold, winter months, a holiday concoction called *Glühwein*. Maria stood over the stove slowly mulling the sweet, red wine with cloves and cinnamon and then served it hot and steaming to ward off the chill for anyone that came in from the cold winter air.

Soon everyone was opening presents and exclaiming over the lavishness of each other's generosity. After the last package had been opened, Maria slipped out of the room only to return with the largest box Lisl had ever seen. Everyone watched as she handed it to the child to open. Her eyes wide with astonishment, Lisl folded back the tissue to unveil the most beautiful doll she had ever seen. She was a three-foot-tall porcelain creation with a delicate face, long eyelashes and beautiful, curly brown hair. To Lisl she was the most gorgeous doll on the face of the earth, and she knew she was to cherish her for years to come.

Christmas was also a deeply religious experience for everyone in the small community. Attending Midnight Mass on Christmas Eve was mandatory. After the opening of presents, everyone dressed up in their holiday finery and walked down to the church together as the bells in the steeple pealed in a joyfully syncopated call to one and all that the celebration of Christ's birth was about to begin. To the Wenzel family, it was the holiest day of the year with the exception of Easter Sunday. The massive pipe organ in the choir loft played all the traditional Christmas hymns including *"Stille Nacht, Heilige Nacht"* and even *"O Tannenbaum."* The congregation sang, and as their voices rang out and drifted out into the clear, starlit night, everyone welcomed the coming of Christ on that magical Holy Eve.

Walking back home from Midnight Mass their footsteps made soft, muffled crunching noises in the snow. Holding tightly to her mother's and father's hands, Lisl closed her eyes and breathed in the cold, night air. The heady fragrance of new-fallen snow mixed with the smoky aroma from dozens of wood-burning stoves would always remain with her as the true essence of Christmas.

CHAPTER 3

The rumblings of the war to come, like distant thunder, became louder and more undeniable as the decade continued in an unstoppable march to destiny. The aftermath of World War I, coupled with the world-wide economic depression, continued to fester and take its toll in German politics through the 1930s. The disastrous implications of the Treaty of Versailles caused major political unrest for a country teetering on the brink of economic collapse and, ultimately, became an opportunity for any fanatical political party to gain a foothold in the ever-weakening Republic. One of these, of course, was the National Socialist German Worker- or Nazi-Party. Like any extremist group, the Nazis appealed to a wide variety of discontented citizens: stalwart nationalists, coarse agitators, unemployed workers, middle-class property owners ever-fearful of a Communist revolution, and the down-trodden in general. Unfortunately, they also relied on a centuries-old theme of discontent — Anti-Semitism. The leader of the Nazi Party, Adolf Hitler, swept into power promising to lead a resurgent Germany to the world power that it once was and more. Elected in 1933 with 37 percent of the democratic vote, Hitler was then installed as Chancellor by the aging Paul von Hindenburg. By the time Paul von Hindenburg died in 1934, Hitler had usurped much of his power and used the subsequent collapse of the Republic to establish a totalitarian regime across the country.

Seemingly overnight in classrooms everywhere pictures of the beloved Paul von Hindenburg were covered with black shrouds. Soon the crucifix that hung on the wall of Lisl's classroom was replaced with a life-sized portrait of Hitler. A vague sense of nervousness colored the mood of the era. The Nazi Party kept the German populace in check with a reign of terror. Nevertheless, schools throughout the province continued the daily prayers that started their morning classes. Through the eyes of a child, Lisl sensed the growing uneasiness as she listened to her parents quietly discussing the political events of the time.

Looking back no one knew then the ramifications of this new German government. Soon churches, labor unions and youth organizations became organs of the State. Even the media — radio, newspapers and the like — were used to control public opinion. Though most of the German citizenry were disturbed by his methods, those who voiced opposition to the new dictator were immediately suppressed by storm troopers or the feared secret police, the Gestapo. Midnight arrests, round-ups and imprisonment soon silenced most of Hitler's opponents. What many people didn't know and modern historians sometimes forget is that the German people were terrorized by the Nazi Party and the dictatorship of Adolf Hitler.

Although the Wenzels were never members of any Home Army as in Poland or an underground Resistance as in France, they did what they could in their modest role as farmers — powerless in the grand scheme of things — yet doing their part in a quiet resistance of sorts to the political events of the time.

With the advent of the war in 1939, food became scarce for everyone, including those lucky enough to live off the land. Even something as basic as the traditional home processing of a hog, once a joyful event, now took on a sinister quality. A government mandate required 80 per cent of any livestock that was processed for food be turned over to the local government, and was then used to feed the military. The mandate was strictly enforced by uniformed officials who made frequent visits to the Wenzel's farm just to count the chickens, geese, hogs, and cattle and keep track of their contributions to the state. Even a certain quantity of eggs had to be turned over to the government. The farm families themselves were not even allowed to keep enough milk to make their own butter. Michael Wenzel soon realized that the meager fruits of his hard labor were ultimately benefiting a government he did not in good conscience support. And so, he eventually sold the farm and all the remaining livestock with it. All that he kept were two acres of land for growing a modest potato crop and a small vegetable garden. Each member of the family pitched in to make ends meet.

Long before the rooster crowed the heralding of a new day, Lisl knew today would a long one. It was the beginning of hops harvesting season and Lisl, now approaching adolescence, spent her summers working alongside other youngster her age in the hops fields harvesting the delicate white hops flowers. As grueling as the work sounded, it was surprisingly quite pleasant.

As the sun peeked over the ridge, the horse-drawn wagon, filled with youngsters eager to earn money for their families, pulled into the yard of the hops farmer.

"We're going to work the south acres today," *Herr* Brandt called as he came hurrying out of the farmhouse to lead the group to the work site.

The early morning air smelled fresh and sweet with the scent of hops blossoms as the workers made their way out into the field. The wagon wheels creaked and groaned under the weight of the laughing boys and girls eager to earn their day's work. They each had baskets by their side and were ready to pluck the fragrant hops. Lisl located her spot as the wagon slowly grinded to a halt in the field and kids scattered up and down the rows to stake out their work site for the day. Lisl always made sure her pals Max, Trudi, and Anthony sat in the same row as she did so that they could sing and talk together while they worked.

It was funny how much they had all grown — how much they had changed, these kids Lisl had known all her life. She supposed she had grown, too. But had she changed as much as these friends? Especially the boys. Lisl stole a glance at Max and Anthony — so tall and strong! It seemed as if both boys had each grown a foot taller since that last day of school. Their legs — so tanned and muscular. Max was even sporting a small nick on his chin that betrayed his attempts to shave even though his face was still baby smooth. Lisl suddenly felt an urge to sit next to the handsome Max, but as she picked up her basket to move over to a spot next to him, she saw that he was jockeying for a position next to Trudi. She sighed. Max was too popular for someone like her. Forget about boys, she told herself, Father said she was too young anyway. Still . . .she wistfully looked over at Max one more time before settling down to begin her work.

The hops vines trailed and grew on long, thin wires leading out from tall poles. The fine wires, loaded heavily with hops blossoms, were often twenty feet high. Once settled on a small stool at the base of a wire, pickers simply pulled the wire down across their lap and then proceeded to pick the flowers off and put them into the basket by their side. Lisl always prided herself on being able to fill at least fifteen baskets before the end of the day. At one mark a basket, fifteen marks for a young girl was an impressive wage.

Soon the breakfast wagon came around with steaming hot rolls and sausages, and then later the lunch wagon with its hearty sandwiches and soups. It was amazing how robust an appetite one developed when working outside for a few hours in the fresh, country air. Later still, dinner was always eaten at the hops farmer's house.

"Well, Lisl, you've done a good job once again," said *Herr* Brandt as he reached for her hand to help her up onto the back of the truck. The twelve-foot long burlap sacks lying on the flatbed were already beginning to bulge with hops from other youngsters. Lisl emptied her baskets into the sacks quickly while the next girl waited for her turn. Feeling the weariness in her muscles, she smiled with the satisfaction of accomplishment and ran to the waiting horse-drawn wagon for the unhurried ride to the farmhouse for their hearty evening meal.

Once harvested, the hops blossoms would then be spread out in a drying room where they were cured, and ultimately sold to local breweries as part of the time-honored recipe for making beer. This harvesting procedure was carried out in the centuries-old tradition over and over again throughout the southern part of the country in spite of war, drought, or famine. To Lisl, it was just one of the many routine activities that she and her family maintained to keep a sense of normalcy in spite of the lunacy of the ever-escalating war.

The winter of '39 was particularly harsh. News of the war brought home stories of many victories, yet the glowing reports from the front did nothing to ease the bitter cold for the citizenry of Altmannstein faced with coal rationing. Snow drifts three meters tall and higher were not uncommon. As she wound her muffler snugly around her neck and pulled on her sturdy boots, Lisl wished now she hadn't agreed to help her friend Berta. At least, not today. It had stopped snowing, but the clouds hung gray and heavy in the winter sky. Berta Stegermeier's father owned a butcher shop, and Berta had to deliver a load of frozen meat on her sled to a farmhouse on the outskirts of town. To escape the boredom of staying inside all afternoon, Lisl had agreed to accompany her friend and help deliver the meat. She trudged down the hill to the *marktplatz* where she and Berta were to meet. Already Lisl could spot Berta's dark figure bundled in wool up to her nose and heading her way. The girl had the ropes of the sled pulled over her shoulder and her plump body was leaning into the wind to pull the meat-laden sled.

"Here, let me give you a hand with that," Lisl offered.

"I didn't know Papa had so much for us to deliver," Berta puffed, her face red with exertion in spite of the cold. She handed one of the ropes to Lisl and the two plodded down the road leading out of town. "Thank goodness the Schneider's farmhouse is not that far, just a few kilometers or so out this way."

The buildings of the town disappeared behind them, and the girls soon found themselves in the snow-covered countryside. They had just stopped to rest when suddenly howling winds whipped up, and snow began to fall once more. Lisl pulled her muffler tightly over her mouth and nose as the fine snowflakes stung her face.

"It's getting worse," Berta yelled over the wind, "maybe we should stop under a tree and rest some more."

"No, we need to keep moving," Lisl puffed grimly.

Thick snow swirled around them in an endless sea of white. "Where are we? I think we're lost!" cried Berta.

Agonizingly exhausted, Lisl sat down on top of the frozen meat. Terror and fatigue overcame her. The Schneider farmhouse was nowhere in sight, and neither of the girls knew which direction to take in the blinding snowstorm.

"We've got to make sure we stay on the road. As long as we stay on the road, we're okay," Lisl said encouragingly. Her hands ached from towing the heavy sled. She pulled off her mittens and looked at her fingers. The tips, now numb, were turning a strange grayish white. She forced herself to flex her fingers in spite of the pain. Keep moving, keep moving, Lisl thought. Don't stop. "Come on, Berta. We can make it. The Schneider house has to be around here some place. I can just feel it!" she persisted. They were now caught in a full-fledged blizzard with nothing but whiteness all around.

"It's hopeless!" Berta cried.

"Come on!" Lisl pushed her friend. "We can't just give up and die!"

Berta began weeping. "I'm so sleepy. Let me just lie here for a while. I just can't go on anymore."

"No! That's the worst thing you can do! Get up! And don't cry. Your tears will freeze around your eyes and make things worse." Lisl tried hard to remember what her father had taught her about survival in a snowstorm, and she knew she couldn't let her friend lie down in the snow. With supreme effort, the two moved slowly against the wind, inching their way down what they felt sure was still the road. As they crested a small rise in the path, the faint gray shape of a farmhouse appeared on the horizon.

A cry of relief rose in her throat, as Lisl pointed to it. "Look! There it is! That's the Schneider's, isn't it?"

"I don't care whose house it is, it's where we're going now!" Berta replied, her eyebrows and nostrils encrusted with ice.

As they trudged stiffly to the house, the golden lights in the window served as a beacon for them.

"What in the world!" *Frau* Schneider exclaimed as she opened the door to the two bedraggled young girls pulling a sled full of frozen meat.

"We got caught in the blizzard," Berta explained. "Papa wanted me to deliver this to you."

"I'm sure your Papa didn't intend for you to come out in this weather, Berta!" *Frau* Schneider scolded. "You girls take off your mittens. I'll get some water."

Soon Lisl and Berta were bundled by the stove, their hands immersed in cool water to gently thaw out their fingertips and counteract the frostbite that had started to set in.

Frau Schneider brewed a pot of hot, steaming peppermint tea as she clucked in a maternal fashion. "Out in this weather! I just can't believe it. You girls could have died! My husband will hitch the horses to the wagon to take you home, but first we'll call your father, Berta, and then he can get word to *Herr* Wenzel that you both are safe." The Schneiders were one of the few farm families with a telephone, and it was not unusual for those with telephones to relay messages to those families without.

Lisl and Berta exchanged sheepish glances, but both were so relieved to be safe and out of the storm.

Toward the end of July 1940, with Germany's many victories on the western front including the taking of the Maginot Line and the subsequent fall of Paris in June, the barracks used to house French P.O.W.'s were soon filled to overflowing. Thus, it became necessary to call upon the rural communities, like Altmannstein and its good citizens, to assist with the war effort by boarding the excess P.O.W.'s. Lisl's family was no different from the countless others receiving their boarders; they made the best of the situation by taking in their assigned prisoner, Henri Prudhomme. Short and slight of build, Henri was at first, a droll little man with incredibly sad, downturned eyes. His first few days in the Wenzel's home were somewhat awkward for everyone, partly because of the language barrier and partly because Henri made it clear from the outset that he had no wish to be in the situation he was in and longed for his home in the province of Burgundy. After a few short weeks of residing with the Wenzel's, however, Henri and Michael became friends of sorts and at least an air of mutual trust and respect seemed to prevail. Maria knitted a pair of Christmas socks for Henri just as she had done for Michael every year, and in return, Henri helped Michael build an incredibly realistic dollhouse that made Lisl the envy of every other young girl in the neighborhood.

Lisl spent many long afternoons in the winter of 1940 playing with her beloved dollhouse often sharing it with one of her friends.

"I can't believe your father and Henri built this gorgeous little house for you. Just look at the tiny furniture," Rosa exclaimed, "everything is so lifelike!"

Knowing that Rosa Weintraub enjoyed the friendship of few youngsters, Lisl had invited the girl over to play. "I know. I'm really lucky. Father told me he was afraid, now that I'm twelve, I might be too grown up for a dollhouse." Lisl ran her hand lovingly over the miniature tiled roof. "But just look at the workmanship. How can anyone not enjoy a work of art like this? Father said Henri spent weeks carving some of these pieces."

"I wish *our* P.O.W. would do something like this for me. André just sits in his room and stares. He's so sullen, he never speaks, and when we try to speak to him, he just stares at us as if he would murder us all if he could. It gives me the shivers."

"Aren't you afraid?" Lisl asked as she rearranged the tiny furniture in the living room.

"No. Well, yes, but Papa put bars around all his windows, and we bring food to him every day. We just won't let him go outside."

"We must be lucky to have Henri then because he's become quite friendly with Father and, if it weren't for this war and the fact that he's our enemy, he'd be quite a decent *mensch*."

"That's one thing André Ravier is not and that's a decent *mensch*! Why, if I didn't know better, I'd swear he was plotting an escape right now."

"Oh, Rosa, are you sure? How do you know?" Lisl asked.

Rosa glanced around quickly as if afraid of being overheard. "He writes things down in French on little bits of paper that he then rolls up and shoves in his pockets. He steals things from the kitchen. My mother was missing a paring knife the other day and, when she asked André if he'd seen it, he just shrugged in that disdainful French way of his! I told Mama we should search his room, but when we did, we never did find it."

"Then how do you know he's taking anything or that he's plotting an escape?" Lisl asked.

Nodding her head slowly, Rosa said, "I just know."

"That would be awful for your family!" Lisl exclaimed in a hushed voice.

"One can never tell about those wily Frenchmen," Rosa said with a sneer, "I hope he stays put until the authorities come to get him again. I know we have to do our part to help in the war effort, but I just wish the military would be able to house these prisoners somewhere other than people's home, if you know what I mean?"

Lisl nodded sympathetically. The girls continued to play with the dollhouse even though each was distracted with her own uneasy thoughts about the Weintraub's strange P.O.W.

Although Henri Prudhomme had finally come to terms with his situation as a P.O.W. and valued his relationship with Lisl's parents, he still missed the native French cuisine so dear to his heart. One spring day in '41, he persuaded Maria to let him prepare an authentic French meal — one that could be enjoyed by the whole family. "Madame Wenzel, I promise you, I will fix a meal that will be *tres magnifique!*" Henri declared, placing the fingertips of his left hand to his lips and kissing them with a resounding smack.

"Very well then, Henri," Maria consented with a hint of a smile, "but I expect my kitchen to be spotless when you finish."

Henri immersed himself in the task of cooking as if he were a man possessed. Vegetables were lightly sautéed; the few pieces of chicken available were prepared for roasting; and greens were tossed for salad.

"I will need some white wine, *s'il vous plait*," Henri asked as he stirred the pots on the stove.

Maria hesitated a moment, then opened the cabinet behind the table and fished out a dusty bottle of Liebfraumilch.

"We've been keeping this for when the war is over," she said, "but I guess you can use some of it now." She reluctantly handed the bottle to him.

Henri looked at the label and sniffed with disdain. "A little sweeter than what's needed, but I guess it'll do," he said.

"Well, it will just have to," Maria retorted pushing a lock of hair from her eyes. "You should be glad we have any wine at all. Besides, I'm not even sure we're going to like your gourmet French dinner all that much anyway."

"Oh, no, *Madame*, you are mistaken. When I am finished, you will think you are eating a slice of paradise."

"I'm not so sure I like having such a cocksure Frenchman tinkering around in my kitchen," she muttered to herself.

And so, the two grumbled good-naturedly and worked side-by-side on the infamous gourmet meal.

At one point, amidst the bustling activity going on in the kitchen, Maria followed Henri out into her garden expecting him to gather more of the tender vegetables that were starting to mature. The garden was small but sufficient with its tidy rows of sprouting lettuce, radishes, onions and carrots. To her complete amazement and disgust, Henri began digging through the soil until he found several fat garden snails which he promptly collected in his pail.

"You're not going to cook those, are you?" she asked incredulously.

"*Mais, oui, Madame*! These *escargots* are almost as succulent as the ones found in my beloved homeland!" Henri answered matter-of-factly, "not only am I going to cook them, but we will all eat and enjoy this wonderful appetizer."

"Henri," she began indignantly as she straightened herself to her full five-foot-four-inch height, "I was a chef in a well-known restaurant in Pfaffenhofen. I cooked many wonderful dishes myself, but I refuse to eat snails!"

Maria watched in disbelief as her strange P.O.W. boarder scrubbed the snails, sautéed them in butter sauce and served them with a flourish as a first course to his dinner!

Once seated at the table the family stared at the black, glistening *escargots* before them. None of them could muster the appetite to try one, although it was apparent from the blissful look on Henri's face that he was thoroughly enjoying his. Later that night, Maria crept back down to the kitchen and scrubbed all the pots and pans again in hot, soapy water. If truth be told, it's not certain whether she ever used the *escargot* pan again.

As peaceful as their coexistence may have been, it was still wartime and, to comply with state regulations, Michael Wenzel was forced to install bars on Henri's bedroom window. However, both men knew it was just for the record. Henri had become almost one of the family and was allowed the freedom to move about and share in family activities.

One Sunday afternoon Anne and Ludwig came for dinner bringing with them some new-found friends, Clara and Thomas Friedrich. The Friedrichs were a young couple that had moved recently into the house next door to Anne and Ludwig. Thomas, a hard-working, earnest young man with a face plain in features, a giant leonine head, and a strong body bred for heavy labor, seemed an odd match for Clara. Thomas's nubile, young wife had a lusty laugh that emitted from full, sensuous lips. Her large, brown eyes missed nothing, and, when she walked, she moved like an animal on the prowl. She had a sharp edge to her and an almost predatory presence. In no time at all, Clara had worked her charm on every man in the room that afternoon, especially Henri, who seemed totally captivated by this brash, blatantly sensual woman.

"*Enchante*," he murmured upon introductions, his lips lightly brushing the back of her hand. All afternoon Henri and Clara stole glances at each other over the rims of their beer glasses while poor Thomas remained oblivious to their growing attraction to each other.

No one could have guessed after that fateful Sunday afternoon how carefully and soundlessly Henri would pry open the bars on his bedroom windows late that night, climb out into the moonlight, then quickly dart into the alley leading up to Clara's house. There a shadowy figure waited for him in the secluded flower garden ready to embrace him and fall to the ground in a lover's tryst.

The dangerous affair between Clara and Henri had not been going on very long when one day, as Lisl was sitting in Dr. Singer's office waiting for a prescription of asthma medicine for her mother, she overheard loud voices in the examining room next door.

"You've got to help me, Doctor, I have no one else to turn to."

Lisl immediately recognized the voice as that of Clara. However, instead of her usual low, sultry voice, this was a desperate, high-pitched cry.

Lisl glanced about the room, trying not to listen. Although sterile in nature, the office had unmistakable human touches: a thriving plant in the corner, a handsomely framed picture of a woman and two children on the desk.

"You're asking me to go against my ethics — everything I stand for, Clara, I can't possibly do that," Dr. Singer's voice stayed calm and controlled.

Lisl was becoming increasingly more uncomfortable as the voices drifted in from the examining room next door.

Clara's voice became even louder and more desperate, "I shall kill myself then, if you won't help me! I can't bear to bring Henri's baby into the world and expect Thomas to rear the child. I would be scorned by everyone for the rest of my life!"

"Please, Clara, try to control yourself," Dr. Singer hissed, "there are patients in the next room."

"I don't care!" she wailed. "You *have* to help me with this — you simply have to!" Suddenly her voice took on a conspiratorial tone, "If you don't, I'll tell everyone in town of our own little affair. I'm sure your wife would be interested to hear about our little late night *tete-a-tetes*."

"Don't be a fool, Clara, no one would ever believe you. I'm the only doctor this town has. People look up to me." Dr. Singer now began sounding a little less calm and controlled. Not daring to breathe, Lisl sat mesmerized by what she was hearing. What was Clara asking Dr. Singer to do? she thought. Lisl tried to draw on her own knowledge of sex, but her thirteen-year-old's hazy expertise was found woefully lacking in the matters of abortion and illicit affairs.

"Nevertheless, I could still make trouble for you. Lord only knows how many other women you took advantage of in the course of your practice," she could hear Clara counter.

In the silence that followed, Lisl's heart thudded loudly in her chest as she realized what was going on.

Finally, she heard Dr. Singer say, "Alright, come back to my office tonight after eight. Irma goes home at seven. As much as I trust her as my assistant, I want to do this alone. The fewer people that know about this, the better."

"Oh, thank you! Thank you, Doctor," Clara's tearful voice shook with relief.

At that moment Irma, Dr. Singer's assistant, came into the room where Lisl was waiting and handed her Maria's prescription. The girl quickly mumbled her thanks and hurried home without saying a word to anyone about the exchange she had just overheard.

A week later she sat in the kitchen of Anne and Ludwig's house watching Anne stir a large kettle of soup. As she ladled some of the soup into a small crock, Anne said, "Lisl, be a dear and take this soup over to Clara. She's sick in bed, and I think this might give her a little strength." Lisl obligingly took the fragrant crock wrapped in a dishtowel to the Heinrich's house and knocked on the door.

A faint voice said "Come in."

Lisl entered the house and took the soup straight to Clara's bedroom. What she saw there made her stop dead in her tracks. Clara was propped up in bed, her exquisite features grotesquely distorted with pain. Her eyes, once lively and sparkling, were sunk deep in their hollows. Most alarming of all was the color of her skin which was tinged a strange yellow hue, as if her face had been brushed with yellow watercolor.

Thomas was by her side gently swabbing her face with a cool cloth. The anguish on his face was heart-rending.

"My darling Clara, please let me take you to the hospital," he pleaded.

"No, no, it won't help. I'll be alright, really I will. Please don't call the hospital," Clara gripped his arm and looked up at him beseechingly. "I promise I'll be all right soon," she whispered hoarsely. "It'll take just a little while for me to get better."

Thomas's face leaned over her. Vertical lines of worry were etched between his eyebrows. He choked back the tears. "All right, Sweetheart, but it's killing me to see you suffer so," he said with a note of resignation.

Clara sighed. Thomas deserved an explanation. She needed the strength to explain; she needed the right words, lots of words, and in the end, what would they say? They would say nothing. How could she possibly explain it all?

"What day is it?" she whispered.

"Sunday."

"Sunday. A day of purity and worship. I suppose I'll burn in hell for this when I die."

"Don't! Don't talk like this. I don't care what happened. I just want you well again," Thomas cried, his voice cracking with emotion.

"Darling, can you ever find it in your heart to forgive me?" Clara squeezed his arm again.

"Forgive? What's there to forgive, Clara? You made a mistake and you're paying for it horribly now. How can I not forgive? You're my wife; we vowed to spend the rest of our lives together no matter what. I can't forget that."

He held her close to him and stroked her hair.

Clara closed her eyes for a moment, and when she opened them again, they were filled with an immeasurable poignant sadness. "My sweet Thomas, you've been so good to me. I never really knew how kind and loving you've always been to me."

"I've always loved you, Clara, and I always will," he answered simply.

With a sigh of resignation Clara said, "I can die in peace now, knowing that even though the Church won't forgive me, at least you have."

Tears streamed from his eyes as Thomas held his beloved Clara. As she watched the heartbreaking scene before her, Lisl then wondered if he knew the whole story.

At that point, she realized that even *she* didn't know the whole story. Walking back to Anne's house, she decided to break her silence and confide in her sister about what she had overheard in the doctor's office.

"Anne," she said, finding her sister in the kitchen wiping down the countertop, "can I talk to you a minute?"

Anne wiped her hands on a dishtowel as she eyed her younger sister warily. Lisl sat down at the kitchen table.

"Do you want me to explain to you about Clara and why she's ill?" she finally asked.

"Yes, and I want to tell you of a conversation I heard a week ago."

As Lisl shared her news with her sister, Anne paused as if the telling would be too painful, and then proceeded to fill in the rest of the story beginning with the sordid affair between Clara and her mystery lover.

With a deep breath, Anne explained that Clara was battling a rampant infection from the abortion that Dr. Singer had performed on her. The infection had already attacked her vital organs, and the yellowish cast of her skin that Lisl had observed that day was the fatal sign of peritonitis.

"No one really knows why someone would take the chances that Clara took. We still don't know who the man is that she had been seeing. She's been keeping that a big secret even though she's gravely ill and could die," Anne mused.

Lisl thought back to the conversation she had overheard in Dr. Singer's office and recalled hearing something about Henri Prudhomme. She started to say something then decided against it. It was not her place to add fuel to the fire. "Wasn't she happy with Thomas? And if not, why did she marry him in the first place?" she asked.

Anne smiled sadly, "Who knows? All I know is she is certainly paying for her sins now."

Lisl wanted to ask more, but her sister's closed, tight face discouraged any more discussion of the taboo subject. Armed with what little knowledge she had, Lisl knew this was all more than someone at the tender age of thirteen could fully comprehend. To think that a skilled and sterile knife could solve a problem of this sort. In the pure, simple and uncomplicated terms of a thirteen year old's world, Lisl could not fathom how a person — man or woman — could make these judgments. That by destroying a life another one can be saved. The irony of it all! Later when the family learned that Henri was

Clara's mysterious lover, the complexity of the situation was heightened even more. For had Clara been forced to have Henri's baby and word of this reached the authorities, Clara surely would have been imprisoned. Yet, still, to take an innocent life... For the first time in her young life, Lisl was keenly aware that there were no easy answers to life's most perplexing problems, and this one was surely one that she was certain she never would understand. If truth be known, she thought, they were all at fault, for having judged Henri and Clara for being the willing victims — pawns as it were — of their circumstances. But Lisl nodded her head knowingly, all the while hating Henri for what he had done to the vivacious and beautiful Clara.

As the days went on, Clara's condition rapidly worsened until Friday of the following week, she died peacefully in Thomas's arms.

A lone church bell tolled slowly as the mourners gathered outside the church the next day to walk the short distance to the town cemetery and lay Clara's body to rest. Thomas, his eyes blinded with grief, followed the priest in the processional. Anne and Ludwig were at his side, their arms linked with his as if physically supporting the grieving giant as they walked. Iron-colored clouds hung heavy in the somber sky. It had rained off and on for most of the day and Lisl's black wool stockings chafed and itched as she walked between her mother and father. In spite of the bone-chilling drizzle, everyone in town had shown up to express their sympathy. Everyone, of course, except the P.O.W., Henri Prudhomme, who sat alone in his room, his face in his hands, weeping silently.

One day, several weeks after Clara's funeral, Michael stopped in at Fischer's Tavern, one of the two pubs facing the *Marktplatz*. Instead of the friendly, noisy atmosphere he expected, Michael was greeted with a hushed silence that hung heavily in the air.

"*Was gibts?*" he asked as Max Fischer motioned him to sit down at a table.

"I'll tell you what's up?" the proprietor said in an agitated voice. "The Weintraubs are gone! Klaus, Sofie, Rosa, all of them — they're all gone!"

"Gone? What do you mean they're gone?" Michael asked as panic rose in his throat.

"Just that! They have disappeared! Yesterday morning when they brought André Ravier, their P.O.W., his breakfast, they found his room empty. The bars on one of the windows had been pried open and, I guess, the prisoner simply escaped. Klaus immediately called *Herr* Krueger to ask what they should do."

"Why Fritz Krueger?" Michael interrupted.

"Because," Max explained with a tone of exasperation, "he's been designated by the *Oberbürgermeister* as our local liaison for all home-boarded P.O.W.'s. Didn't you know that?"

"Are you sure?" Michael asked suspiciously. He himself had been in touch with the local magistrate during Henri Prudhomme's tenure with the Wenzels and had never heard of any change in the line of authority.

"Yes, yes — *Herr* Krueger told us that himself. Now let me finish the story. Well, the Weintraubs didn't have to worry long about what would happen. My wife didn't see Sofie at the butcher shop this morning and so went to their house to see if they were alright. Michael, I tell you it was the strangest thing; everything was left as if they had just gone for a short walk. Dishes were on the table; a book was lying open on the couch, but the family was nowhere to be found. Something terrible has happened to them; I just know it." This last sentence was uttered in a frightened whisper.

"We need to stay calm, Max. I'm sure they've simply been taken in for questioning." Michael said fighting the cold, raw fear that was paralyzing him now.

"No — no, Michael, don't you understand? They've all been taken to a detention camp. They may not ever be back!" Max whispered hoarsely, his eyes wet with emotion. He produced a handkerchief from his trouser pocket and blew his nose loudly. Klaus Weintraub was Max's wife's cousin and the two families had been close for many years.

Michael couldn't help but think of his own P.O.W., Henri Prudhomme, and the bars on his window. How many times had he, Michael, let Henri outside to help with work in the fields? Surely

Henri wouldn't try to escape the Wenzel's home! Of course, reason told him, a good P.O.W.'s duty is to try to escape as much as possible. The prudent thing to do now was to go home right away and check the bars for tightness. Yes, that would make him feel much better.

Michael murmured hasty good-byes to his friends at the pub and hurried home just in time to find a local inspector at the Wenzel's door. Just a routine inspection of the security system for our P.O.W.'s, the official smiled, nothing to get upset about. Michael nervously assured him that everything was in order and led the official up to Henri's room for inspection. To Michael's shocked dismay, the bottom portion of the bars had been partially sawed in half. Henri was safely in the kitchen with Maria, but it was quite obvious, that the French P.O.W. intended to make his escape any day now. Michael quickly realized what grave danger he and his family were truly in. After the Weintraubs' disappearance, such shocking events would now be merely whispered about in taverns and shops for, these days, no one could afford to speak too loudly of the misfortunes of neighbors lest the same misfortune might befall them.

Someone, however, in the local magistrate's office took kindly to the Wenzel family. With a few changes in the paperwork accompanied by the right signatures, Michael and his family were spared imprisonment. The next day Michael was called to the magistrate's office and was told that, although the Wenzels would continue to keep their prisoner, Henri would be picked up at the end of each day for incarceration in a local barracks and brought back to their house each morning for his day's labor. A few months later, Henri Prudhomme was picked up from the Wenzel's house, transferred to an undisclosed determent camp, and was never heard from again. Thomas Friedrich went on to marry a seventeen-year- old, apple-cheeked girl from a nearby farm, and together they reared three healthy children.

News of the war seemed to bode well for Germany. Hitler had invaded Russia and was met with surprising success in spite of the intensity of the Russian counteroffensive. With the Japanese attack on Pearl Harbor, the United States entered the war, and in late December, 1941, Hitler boldly declared war on the United States. Full-scale battles raged now on every front, and for the German Reich, victory was well within reach.

One crisp Sunday evening in January, Michael entered his favorite pub and hailed his card-playing friends with a friendly *"Grüss Gott"* as he tossed his hat on the hat rack.

"What kind of greeting is that?" Fritz Krueger looked up from his cards and called out to him. Fritz owned an ice-cream store in town and as a long-time merchant in Altmannstein, he had always been taken with his own importance. Now as a local Party representative, he flaunted his position to his friends.

Michael turned around to size up his old friend. "Why, it's the proper greeting for friends," he replied as he took his place at the table.

"Not anymore, it isn't," *Herr* Krueger snapped. "When you come into a room, you hold your hand up high and say 'Heil Hitler!' *That* is the proper greeting in the New World Order."

"Maybe for you, but it isn't for me," Michael said quietly, "now let's just play some cards, shall we?"

From that day forward, Michael Wenzel stopped patronizing that tavern and moved to a friendlier pub down the street.

The war was hitting closer to home now than ever before when, within days of each other, Lisl's sisters announced tearfully that their husbands had received their draft notices. The oldest sister Maria's husband Franz was already in the Navy. Now Ludwig was going into the Army, and Frieda's husband Alfons was headed for the *Luftwaffe*, the German Air Force. The war had truly reached Lisl's front door.

CHAPTER 4

June 1943, and the war was in full scale, appearing to rage on forever. Germany had been invaded from both the East and the West with air attacks as well as ground assaults. In the town of Altmannstein, the news of a neighbor or loved one perishing in battle was now commonplace. Furthermore, it seemed as if all around the community, military draftees were getting younger and younger. The war had truly hit home. Light-armored cars followed by Schmeisser-armed motorcycle flanked convoys of military lorries that now routinely rolled through the streets of Altmannstein. Children laughed and chickens squawked in a flurry of feathers to get out of the way of the supply-laden trucks, their canvas covers stretched tightly over high bows.

"Where is Stefan being sent, do you know?" Lisl was sitting in Trudi's room as the two girls worked on their embroidery together.

"He's going to Berlin for his training. That will only last three weeks. From there he will be stationed somewhere near France or Belgium, I don't know. Don't ask me. He's pretty closed-mouthed about it, that's all I can say. I'm sure whatever he'll be doing will be terribly important to the cause." Trudi kept her dark eyes downcast to conceal her anguish and maintain the abruptness that protected her from hurt. Her older brother, Stefan, was one of the last of the eighteen-year-olds in Altmannstein to receive his draft notice. He and Lisl had just started taking long romantic walks together on weekends. Trudi had been teasing Lisl about being sweet on her brother and now, he was in his room packing and getting ready to go to war.

"My brother-in-law Ludwig is stationed in France," Lisl said. "He's always sending home French-made shoes to Anne and me. Of course, we can't wear them all so we barter them for eggs, flour, or even clothes when we can. Maybe Stefan will send you something nice from France."

"Huh! If he sends anybody anything, it'll be to you. We all know how he feels about you."

If only you knew how I feel about him, Lisl thought. Her heart ached at the thought of this wonderful, young man going off to war. "Well, I know we will all miss him," was all she could manage with the lump in her throat. What a banal phrase! Was that all she could say? This handsome young man who's such an important part of her life now — and all she could say is "we will all miss him?" Why couldn't she pour out what was really in her heart? Funny how someone you've known all your life, who's been there at every turn, whom you've almost taken for granted, suddenly turns into Mr. Wonderful. Lisl and Stefan had practically grown up together. As Trudi Hofer's older brother, Stefan was always in the background of Lisl's life — sometimes as a guardian angel for the two girls, but more often than not, as a nuisance to them. Then one day — she really couldn't recall how or when it happened — Stefan changed in Lisl's eyes. He was no longer the pesky brother always playing tricks on Trudi and her. He was worldly, handsome, and he melted her heart when he smiled at her.

Stefan stuck his head in the doorway. "Lisl, promise you'll take a walk with me after dinner this evening. My train leaves tomorrow, and I want to spend my last evening with you."

"Mama won't like that, Stefan," Trudi threatened with a scowl, "you better plan to spend your last evening at home with your family."

"Don't worry," Stefan laughed as he pulled Trudi's hair, "I'll be home in time to sit with everyone for a while."

Later that evening Lisl strolled hand-in-hand with Stefan and listened to him voice his fears. "I should be pretty excited about going into the *Luftwaffe*. They said if I learn quickly enough and pass my exams, I can go straight to flight school and learn to be a fighter pilot. I have to admit, it does sound exciting, but, honestly, Lisl, I'm more scared than excited. My true love has always been art. You know that. I've always abhorred fighting of any kind. Our government has gone mad with this New World Order and *Deutchland über alles*. I know to say these things is almost treason — especially for a new soldier, but I know I can say these things to you. I feel I can trust you, Lisl."

Lisl looked up at his handsome face. He was dark-haired like his sister, but that's where the similarity ended. Unlike Trudi's beefy farm-girl face, Stefan had the finely-chiseled features of an artist or poet. His hands were delicate with long, graceful fingers that were meant to hold a brush or pen. One would never envision him holding a gun or fighting duels to the death in the sky. Lisl wondered if he would have the toughness and fortitude to survive the battlefield.

"So, Lisl, will you give a new soldier a little good-bye kiss?" They had stopped to rest at a bench under an old chestnut tree. The sun was setting behind the hills and the air glowed golden around the two lovers.

Lisl turned her face up to his and he tenderly kissed her lips.

"Oh, Stefan, I will pray every night for your safe return," she cried softly. They held each other for a few moments.

"You can write to me, you know," he said eagerly. He took both her hands in his. "The mail delivery to the front is still pretty reliable. I won't be able to tell you much about where I am or what I'm doing, but to be able to hear from you would mean everything to me!"

Suddenly there was no other world but theirs. He reached out and pulled Lisl close. They kissed again and then clung to each other like two lost children in a storm. Lisl cried into his neck, and he stroked her hair slowly.

"I won't be able to bear it if anything happens to you," Lisl whispered through her tears.

"I love you, Lisl. . . I love you. . ." His words caressed her as he gazed into her eyes, then kissed the tears from her lashes.

Soon they realized it was getting late, and he had promised his family that he would spend some time with them. Neither one of them spoke as he walked Lisl back to her house.

Lisl felt sure her heart would never mend as Stefan kissed her good-bye once more before disappearing into the darkness.

After two months of training, Stefan soon began writing long, yearning letters to Lisl.

August 4, 1943,

Liebe Lisl,

You will be so proud of me when you hear that I not only graduated at the top of my class in flight school, but I am scheduled to be one of the few fighter pilots to fly the new ME 262. This is the first jet fighter in the world! It's built by the Messerschmitt factory, and it can go two hundred forty kilometers per hour faster than anything the Allies have in the sky. And your Stefan will be in the cockpit!

As part of my training I was privileged yesterday to witness a momentous occasion in history: the test launching of our V-2 rocket. This has been a top secret project of the Reich's for some time now, and although none of us knew exactly what this new weapon would do, we knew that it was the premiere secret weapon for the Reich and it would change the way we do battle forever. It is a "robot bomb," and I am told it flies up to fifty miles in altitude and can reach a speed of 3,400 mph! Imagine, Lisl, a weapon that can go that far and that fast! It was fortunate for us that we discovered it before the Americans. I am proud that my country was able to develop the technology for such a powerful weapon first. Perhaps it will help us win this war and then, hopefully, all the killing will stop, we will have peace again, and I can come home to you, my darling Lisl.

I can't tell you where I'll be fighting because the censors won't let me tell much more than this, and as it's almost dinnertime, I will close for now. Keep me in your prayers. I think of you often.

Lovingly yours,
Stefan

Lisl pressed the letter to her chest and felt tears of pride sting behind her eyes. She *was* proud of him, and she would write to him often.

August 6, 1943
My dear Stefan,

Yes, I am so very proud of you. I visualize you in the cockpit of that new jet fighter and my heart swells with pride. Please, please, please, stay safe, however. I do worry about you, you know. Each night I get on my knees and pray by your picture — Mama thinks I'm silly for "mooning" over your picture the way I do, but I can't tell her how very much I'm in love with you. Your letters mean so much to me. Every week I race to the post office to see if there is a letter from you. Please take care of yourself.

With love,
Your Lisl

October 20, 1943
Liebe Lisl,

It's only been three months since I've been here and already I'm sick to death of what I've experienced. You recall that V-2 bomber test launching that I wrote to you about recently. Our squadron leader informed us that less than two weeks after our visit, Peenemünde was attacked by a fleet of RAF night bombers. This ancient port city on the Baltic had been the secret location of the research and development facility for those revolutionary V-1 and V-2 bombers. The entire factory and laboratory facilities in Peenemünde were destroyed. Lisl, almost two hundred of Deutchland's top minds were obliterated in that attack, including Dr. Walter Thiel and his chief engineer Erich Walther. What a waste! Dr. Thiel was regarded as one of our country's most brilliant scientists. The ideas and the technology to implement those ideas are now lost, perhaps forever. I know it is naive of me to even think this way, but the dreamer in me wishes that instead of destroying those brilliant minds, mankind could have harnessed their collective expertise for the good, rather than the destruction of human lives. What a different world there might have been then!

Right now they have me in ground action for a while because we're advancing deeper into France and we need all the manpower we can muster. *Mein Liebling*, I am not the same man that kissed you good-bye that bright summer day last June. I've seen more men get killed in the few short months I've been at the front than any one person needs to see in a lifetime. I know that I will never again be the same innocent young man you knew. Lisl, I've aged a hundred years since you've seen me, not so much in appearance but in my soul. My buddies and I live in a constant world of horror and death and I've discovered that, in spite of my training, I don't deal well with the killing. Just today I saw something I hope I'll never have to see again. One of our panzers took a direct hit from a mortar round. Some of us who saw it ran over just as the officer in charge was trying to scramble out of the turret. We ran over to where he lay and saw that his face was on fire as well as his arms and chest. He was still alive and trying to tell us something, so we quickly rolled him in the grass and put out the flames with a blanket. He died a few minutes later, nevertheless. I'll never forget the sight of his face in flames while he was trying to talk. It's images like this that will haunt me the rest of my life. Even if I get out of all this alive, I'll be as much of a victim as the countless men who have given their lives on both sides of the war. Remember me the way I was before and pray for me.

Lovingly Yours,
Stefan

Lisl cried as she read the lines. She cherished all of Stefan's letters, bundling them, tying them together with a pink ribbon and placing them safely in her chest-of-drawers. She kept his picture in a little silver frame by the side of her bed and kissed it before going to sleep. She prayed every night for his safe return.

It was a quiet, snowy afternoon in November when Anne burst through the door of the Wenzel home and ran crying to Maria's side.

"It's Ludwig — they got him!" she sobbed.

Lisl's heart stood still as she visualized her beloved brother-in-law cut down in the throes of battle.

"Got him? What do you mean 'they got him,' Anne?" Maria asked holding her daughter by the shoulders.

"He's been wounded and captured," Anne replied as she took a handkerchief from her pocket and wiped her eyes.

Lisl and Maria exchanged relieved glances. "Captured? Oh, thank God he's just captured. I was afraid you meant he had been killed," Maria said gently pushing a lock of Anne's hair off her tear-stained face. "It'll be alright, *Liebchen*. The Allies, from what Alfons has written, take good care of their P.O.W.s."

Frieda's husband had recently been captured as well. It was the Russians who, according to all reports, were not honoring the Geneva Convention with humane treatment of their prisoners. Horror stories of the barbaric brutalities German prisoners suffered at the hands of their Russian captors abounded throughout the community. When word came of a neighbor's son or husband being captured in battle, the first words on everyone's lips were " Which front did he fight in?" If the answer was the "eastern front" sympathy poured from the hearts and compassion welled in the eyes of those who knew the unfortunate soldier.

"I know, Mama. It's just that he's been wounded. And — and — I don't know how badly, or if he's suffering right now. Oh, how will I be able to live?" This last wail brought on a fresh torrent of tears.

"Does it say where he was captured?" Lisl asked pointing to the crumpled letter in Anne's hands.

"Only that he's somewhere in France. His last letter said something about a big, secret offensive somewhere in the Ardennes Forest. So, I suppose, that's where he was wounded and captured," Anne replied, heaving a ragged breath and drying her tears.

"Anne, listen to me," said Maria firmly, "you have got to be brave. We've all got to be brave. You must not give up hope. Pray for your husband every day. He'll come home to us again. Ludwig's a survivor. He's strong, he's resourceful, and he thinks on his feet. He will come out of this alive. And when he and Alfons, too, come home from this horrid war, we will have our family back together again. We simply can't give up hope." She took a hard look at Anne as she spoke. "Promise me you won't give up hope — promise?"

Anne gave her mother a weak smile. "I promise," she whispered.

The three women sat together taking comfort in each other's

presence. The snow piled silently on the window ledge outside as the clock ticked the minutes away.

As Christmas approached, Lisl received one more letter from Stefan.

Dec. 12, 1943
Liebe Lisl,
I can't believe that Christmas is in less than two weeks. I wish I were there with you. The snow is bitterly cold here, and I long for the warmth of your arms around me. Tomorrow we fight somewhere near Belgium. At last I'll be able to fly my plane again. I like fighting from the air so much better than on the ground. Somehow, it seems less personal. We concentrate on targets. Roll and dive. Sometimes we fly so close, I can see the faces of the enemy in the cockpits as we're shooting at each other, but most of the time, they are just impersonal targets. It's the only way I've found I can detach myself from the killing. Otherwise, I would quickly go mad. Our goal is to capture Antwerp so that we can cut off the supplies to the Allies. Wish me luck, Lisl.

I will try to write again soon. In the meantime, *Frohe Weihnachten*, my darling Lisl. Have a wonderful Christmas and remember me in your prayers.
Lovingly yours,
Stefan

Lisl was at Trudi's house when the dreaded telegram came. The girls had been helping Trudi's mother with some Christmas baking when they heard a knock at the door. Opening the door slowly and seeing the uniformed telegram messenger standing there, Trudi's mother almost collapsed. "No, no! Go away! I know what you have! It's a lie, a lie! It can't be true! Oh, God, it can't be true!" she screamed.

The messenger had seen countless mothers, wives and sisters react this way, and each time he hated the job that he had to do.

Sometimes even the fathers, especially the old ones, would get tearful. He felt the gut-wrenching pain as he watched the women's faces turn from the brief smiling politeness to awareness and then horror when they recognized him as the messenger of doom that he was. It never got easier. Quickly, he handed her the envelope along with the small package he was assigned to deliver, then got on his bicycle and sped away, brushing away his tears roughly with the back of his hand.

The telegram from the *Wehrmacht* High Command started with "We regret to inform you that your son, Stefan Hofer, has been killed in action. His plane was shot down over Antwerp, Belgium, and caught fire before he could safely eject. Please take comfort in the fact that he died a noble death while serving his country. In honor of his bravery, the Third Reich wishes to present to him, posthumously, the Iron Cross, Deutschland's highest award for valor and bravery. Our sympathies are with you and your family." It was known that the Iron Cross was one of the highest military honors bestowed on a German soldier.

Stefan's mother opened the box and slowly removed the heavy silver medallion from its velvet pouch. Her eyes glistened with tears as she held up the medal. "I gave birth to this child and nurtured him for eighteen years. For what?? Just so the Fatherland can take him away from me and give me this — this — this trinket in return?" she sobbed. She flung the medal across the room. "What good is this cold piece of metal when I don't have my son any more, I ask you!"

Trudi quietly retrieved the Iron Cross from the floor and stared at it in her hands. Then she slowly walked over to hold her mother as the older woman sobbed in her arms.

"Let me have it back," her mother cried. She clutched the medal to her chest and crumpled to the floor in a sorrowful wail as Trudi knelt over her in a futile attempt to comfort the stricken woman.

Later after Trudi's mother had taken to her bed with a cup of tea, Lisl and Trudi sat quietly in the little living room and hugged each other as silent tears streamed down their faces.

Christmas, 1943, was a quiet one for Altmannstein. With the war still raging and deaths being mourned all over little village, no one was in much of a festive mood. Lisl just wanted to get the holidays over with and hope for a better year. She had read and re-read Stefan's letters over and over and walked around performing her usual chores as if in a daze. One bleak January afternoon, she went to the dresser and picked up an old snapshot of the two of them. It had been taken during a festival the previous spring. She studied their grainy images in the picture. How young they both looked! Her face glowed with innocent happiness and the vigor of youth. Everything was round — round cheeks, round eyes, round mouth — all so young and cherubic. She glanced up and caught her reflection in the dresser mirror. The difference was astonishing! Her face was so much more angular now — her cheekbones were prominent — her eyes reflected a vague sadness now. Is this what grieving does to a person? Or is it just part of growing up? No, she thought, she had already experienced more tragedy than most young girls her age. If only Stefan had lived — then she could be happy. Perhaps they would have married. I would have made you a good wife, Stefan, she thought. But when you died, a little of me died with you. She sighed. What more would life hold for her? She had to go on living, and she knew in her heart of hearts, that eventually she would. She felt lucky to have known such a kind and gentle person like Stefan for the little time that they had together, but she knew that she would never be the same again.

During the last and desperate months of the war, Hitler declared an emergency proclamation that called on all males between the ages of sixteen and sixty who were able to carry arms to prepare themselves to defend their own town or village if needed — the *Volkssturm* or Peoples Army it was called. Historically, it was the beginning of the end. In the grand scheme of Hitler's desperate war, even girls were not exempt from duty of some sort. In conjunction with this program, it was decreed that girls over the age of fifteen would work one year — a "duty year" in servitude of a household.

Now sixteen, Lisl was scheduled to attend a parochial school in Regensburg. Michael and Maria searched desperately for a way for their daughter to continue her schooling uninterrupted while meeting her State obligation to work. Therefore, the practical thing to do was to find room and board where she could quietly serve out this duty year while finishing her schooling.

The Wenzels considered themselves fortunate to find a kindly, older couple who had been childless all their lives and who needed help running their dairy store in Regensburg. The room they provided Lisl was right above the store, and so it became the girl's duty to wait on customers after school and then lock up in the evenings. Each night after closing, she would wearily climb the stairs to her room and do her homework. Although tiring, the schedule seemed to fit her perfectly, so she quickly settled into the routine.

Having never been away from home before, the girl sometimes grappled with bouts of homesickness. Although *Herr* and *Frau* Weber were kind to her and treated her like a daughter, she longed for home, familiar surroundings and friends her own age. The loneliness was eased somewhat when one of the store's regular customers, *Frau* Meiers befriended her. The young mother of two little boys, Irene Meiers was herself somewhat lost while her husband, Josef, was off fighting on the German front-line. The two young women quickly became fast friends often taking long walks together on Sundays.

"Helmut, be careful with your brother — he's only two, you know," Irene cried, as she and Lisl sat in a nearby park one Sunday watching her boys play.

"I know, Mama, I won't let him fall," the older boy replied as he struggled to keep the giggling toddler on his back. The boys were playing horse-y and it was all little Helmut could do to keep his husky, baby brother balanced on his back as they romped in the grass. Inevitably, both boys fell on the ground in a fit of laughter.

With a wistful smile, Irene shook her head and said, "I wish Josef was home. He's missing out on so much with the boys. The baby is putting new words together every day, and Helmut is doing so well in kindergarten." Her voice cracked as she whispered, "And *I* miss him, too."

Lisl gazed up at her gentle, gray eyes that were now filled with tears and her heart ached for this brave, young woman. The luminous waves of her honey-colored hair gave Irene a soft air of innocence. Lisl suspected she was not more than 5 or 6 years older than she, so to the young Lisl, she was like a beautiful older sister reminding her of her own older sister Maria. At that moment she would have given anything to be able to bring Irene's beloved Josef home to her.

"I hate this war and what it does to people! Surely it can't go on much longer," Lisl cried fiercely as she turned her eyes back to the children.

"No, you wouldn't think so," Irene said with a sigh. "Although Josef writes that the bombing will get worse, even for us, before it's all over. Ever since the Allies invaded Normandy, France this past June, he says he's observed a withering of spirit in his comrades. It's as if they sense defeat and just can't go on anymore."

Instinctively, both women stared down the street to where the newly dug bunkers stood, silent and empty now as if waiting to enfold and protect the townspeople at the next wail of the sirens. Lisl jumped up to shake off the ponderous gloom that hung over both of them.

She pulled Irene to her feet and said, "Let's go. It's getting dark."

They gathered the children together and silently trudged home.

In the weeks that followed she saw Irene as often as possible — sometimes helping with the boys who, although never unruly or rambunctious, could at times be a handful. Lisl always brought a little something for them whenever she could. Food was strictly rationed by then, and it seemed as hard as Irene tried to hold everything together, there was never enough.

Irene's husband, Josef, was apparently right: the bombings became more frequent and more intense. The Allies were apparently bent on destroying every living thing in Germany. Lisl and the Webers each kept a suitcase packed — always at the ready — for one of the many trips to the bunkers that served as bomb shelters.

The first time the air raids sounded their warning, Lisl was fast asleep.

"Lisl! Get up! Hurry! We have to run! The bombs are coming!" *Frau* Weber burst into Lisl's room and shook the sleeping girl.

"My suitcase is already packed, *Frau* Weber," Lisl murmured as she quickly slipped into her shoes and hurried out the door with the older woman. The sounds of distant explosions filled the air. As Lisl and the Webers rushed into the bunker, Lisl could almost taste the raw fear that gnawed at her insides. They quickly found vacant places on one of the many long benches that lined the bomb shelter. People from all over the neighborhood were streaming in with their belongings, sad little bundles of clothing, a few precious heirlooms — silver candlesticks and such, every now and then a wide-eyed child clutching a puppy or cat. The bunker smelled faintly of wet dirt mixed with the human smells of dozens of people in damp wool clothing. Lisl hugged herself and prayed. Oh, how she longed for her mother! She wanted with all her heart to be in Altmannstein right now. She didn't belong in Regensburg. She couldn't understand how this year of servitude could help her country's war effort. All it was doing now was putting her in harm's way. She wanted the war to end and she didn't care who won, as long as the bombing stopped! The incessant thundering outside shook the bunker violently. Lisl looked up to see a fine stream of dirt sifting here and there from the ceiling. The bare light bulbs blinked as they swayed from the tremors. Suddenly the lights went out and people screamed. Lisl and the Webers held each other tightly until, finally, mercifully, the bombing stopped and the official at the door declared it safe to go back outside. This was to become a routine event for the next few weeks, and each time was just as terrifying as the last.

 One bright afternoon in late October, Lisl finished early with school and rushed home to help *Frau* Weber in the store. Milk was being rationed out that day, and the store was particularly crowded. The girl busied herself behind the counter when she heard the tinkling of the bell above the door signaling yet another customer waiting to be served. Glancing up she saw it was Irene and her children.

 Lisl rushed over to her and whispered, "Don't leave yet. I have something for you." Irene looked puzzled, but Lisl winked conspiratorially and continued with the other customers.

 "Please call again," she smiled as she ushered the last customer to the door. Wiping her hands on her apron, Lisl could hardly contain herself as she led Irene to the back of the store.

"Here," she said, shoving a container of milk at her, "it's the rest of my ration, and I don't need it."

"Oh, Lisl," she exclaimed, her eyes growing wide, "you're the best friend a person could ever have!"

Milk was by now so carefully rationed: only one-eighth of a liter was allowed per person. This amount was roughly the equivalent of six ounces. She held the precious milk in her hands, and Lisl could see the gratitude in her eyes. Gratitude and something else — was it sorrow or foreboding? she couldn't tell. It was only when Irene turned to leave that she stopped and hesitated near the door.

"What's wrong, Irene?" Lisl asked searching her lovely face for a clue.

"Lisl," she said, lowering her eyes to the floor, her voice barely audible, "I got a letter from Josef yesterday. I had told him about you and how kind you've been to me and our boys. He wrote that he is praying for all of us and is so worried about our safety."

As Irene walked out the store, she stopped in the doorway and said, "May God bless you and keep you well." Then turning on her heels, she hurried down the steps. Lisl felt a shiver run up her spine as Irene's words echoed in her ears. "May God bless you and keep you well."

She quickly locked the door and ran up to her room just as the air raid sirens began their piercing wail. Her heart grew heavy with a mysterious sense of foreboding.

"May God bless you and keep you well." Why would Irene say that to her this time?

"Come quickly, Child," *Frau* Weber urged as she and her husband stood downstairs in the hallway waiting for her. Lisl couldn't shake the ominous feeling as she grabbed her suitcase and ran with the Webers across the street to the bunker. The bomb shelter was filling up rapidly. At the entrance she paused a moment and looked up at the sky. Headed towards them all was a squadron of Allied bombers flying in a low "V" formation and flanked by tight formations of Republic P-47's Thunderbolts fighter escorts. In the next second the sky became a solid, gray canopy of bombs raining down on them.

Little did any of the people in the civilian community realize why the war was hitting perilously close to home. In reality, the Allies, specifically the U. S. Army Air Force 8th Bomber Command, was focusing on not only the systematic destruction of all German war plants and communications networks, but also the invasion of the continent in order to set up a second front as it were. The first of these strikes came in early Spring of 1943 as Allied bombs wiped out the Foche-Wulfe factory in Bremen and the ball-bearing plant in Schweinfurt, and continued deeper and deeper into Germany for the next two years as key cities became strategic targets for the 8th Bomber and 8th Fighter Commands. The Messerschmitt factory near Regensburg cranked out hundreds of ME-109 fighter planes critical to the success of the German *Luftwaffe* and was, therefore, high on the Allies' hit list. In August 1944, Regensburg had become the target of the Eighth Air Force's most ambitious offensive of the war. One hundred forty-seven B-17s, commonly known as Flying Fortresses, escorted by a squadron of P-47 Thunderbolts, pounded the city and its surrounding territory in hopes of destroying the critical Messerschmitt factory. After aerial reconnaissance pictures showed that very little damage to the factory had been done, another massive attack was launched — this one culminating the end of what was to be known as Big Week, a week of major victories and successful strikes against the heartland of Germany.

It was not surprising, then, that the gray canopy Lisl saw coming towards her that infamous day in October 1944, was 298 tons of bombs dropped from hundreds of B-17s and B-24s. Scrap metal and flak were flying through the air, and she quickly ducked down into the bunker. Fear gripped her heart in icy tentacles as she searched the darkened chamber for Irene and her sons. Neighbors, acquaintances, and customers from the diary store streamed in. All around her men, women and children were huddled together to pack in as many people as the bunker could hold. Old men with stoic faces, small children, their eyes large and fearful, and old women in black shawls fingering their rosaries as they silently mouthed their prayers. How could the bunker hold so many people? With wall-to-wall bodies, Lisl felt the stifling closeness and wanted to scream. Everyone in their neighborhood seemed to be there. Everyone, that is, except Irene and her boys.

"Oh, please let them be here," she prayed. "God bless them and keep them well," she whispered to herself over and over until she finally spotted them rushing in — the last ones to enter before the heavy door was lowered shut. Her knees weak with relief, she thanked God that they had made it into the bomb shelter.

The sirens wailed nonstop in a shrieking warning of the muffled thunder of bombs hitting their targets outside. The bombing continued relentlessly for what seemed like an eternity. Was there anything left outside to destroy? Lisl thought. Why couldn't they just stop? Please, God, make them stop this madness. She squeezed her eyes shut and covered her ears to the deafening noises. Suddenly with a flash of light, an incredible force ripped open the bunker. And then, as if in slow motion, she sensed her body being thrown into mid-air like a rag doll. The cool air was mixed with heat, smoke, deafening screams and blinding white light. She felt the heart-lurching sensation of a roller coaster ride out of control plummeting to the depths of despair. Get off, get off, she thought, before it's too late. Don't let this take over. She must be strong. Her mind reeled. She must will herself, in the face of the turmoil around her, to be strong. And then. . . just as suddenly, nothing. Black, silent nothingness.

Strange voices muffled like tiny sound waves over snow, thick and insulating snow buzzed in her head. Strange and remote whiteness around her. Everything was powder-white and quiet.

The old man in the blood-stained uniform shuffled slowly down the busy hospital corridor. All around him the wounded were lined up along the tiled walls waiting for treatment from the precious few doctors and nurses who were scurrying from room to room and from hall to hall trying to be in a hundred places at one time. The injured, mostly women and children, numbered in the hundreds. Clothing ripped, limbs gashed open, faces charred and blistered from fire, they sat. Some stoically silent, others crying and screaming for release from the pain. Particularly heart-wrenching were the sad wails of the children, confused children looking for their mothers, and toddlers who were now orphans and had nowhere to turn. Everywhere confusion. Finally the old man reached a nurse bending over a patient in a crowded ward.

"Can you direct me to *Fräulein* Wenzel, please?" he asked as the nurse pulled the sheet over the unseeing eyes of the unfortunate woman lying there.

"Come with me," she replied wearily, "I'll take you to her."

"*Fräulein* Wenzel. . . *Fräulein* Wenzel. . ." As if from far away a soft voice echoed in the recesses of her brain. Lisl struggled to make sense of it. Slowly she opened her eyes to see a nurse's face smiling down at her. Suddenly she was aware. She was in a hospital ward. She stared at the nurse's starched white cap, the smell of alcohol assaulting her nostrils, and murmured weakly, "What happened?"

"You're a lucky girl," she said. "There's an older gentleman here to see you. He's been most worried about you and, if you're strong enough, I'll let him in to see you."

Lisl stared hard at her face and tried to think.

"Oh, yes," she whispered hoarsely, expecting to see *Herr* Weber. She tried to sit up, but soon realized her face and arms were encrusted with mud and sand.

"Hello, Little One." The nurse ushered in the weary-looking man dressed in a blood-spattered uniform.

"*Herr* Kohler!" the young girl cried. "What are you doing here?" It was her old music teacher from home.

"God was with you for sure," he solemnly replied. Too old to be drafted into the military, *Herr* Kohler was assigned to a clean-up crew as a director. With bombing as heavy as it was throughout this part of the country, *Herr* Kohler and men like him were never wanting for work. Apparently, he had been assigned to Regensburg, and so after each bombing, he would routinely look for Lisl to make sure she was all right. He would then telephone his wife back in Altmannstein, and she would convey the message to Maria and Michael that their youngest was safe.

"Are you strong enough for me to tell you what happened?" He asked holding her hands in his.

"Yes, of course."

Xavier Kohler gazed sadly at the girl staring up at him from the hospital bed. Her hair was matted with blood and dirt. Her face and arms were still encrusted with sand and mud from the demolished bunker. A bandaged gash on her scalp, although hastily cleaned and covered by an attending doctor, was already soaked and dripping blood on her shoulder. I owe it to Michael and Maria to take care of this child, he thought. She had been his brightest pupil during happier days in Altmannstein. He had marveled at how quickly Lisl was able to learn the intricacies of the accordion and not only memorize the standard scales and chords, but quickly came up with her own nuances to the music he taught and gave it a style of her own. A child with that much talent needed sheltering. He vowed to protect her now at all costs.

Drawing a heavy breath, he continued, "This particular bombing was extraordinarily heavy. The bunker you were in held eighty people and only seven including yourself came out alive. I looked endlessly amidst the rubble for you, Lisl. Finally I ran to where a pile of bodies lay heaped one on top of another and I spotted a hand. I recognized the garnet ring your godmother gave you and knew it was your slender hand. I rushed over to feel your pulse. It was rapid and faint, but at least I knew you were still alive. So I quickly commanded my men to get you out of the pile and lift you onto the wagon." Ignoring another air raid alert, he said, *Herr* Kohler then drove on to deliver Lisl to the hospital.

"What about *Frau* Meiers and her boys and *Herr* and *Frau* Weber?" Lisl asked anxiously searching his eyes for the answer that in her heart she already knew.

Herr Kohler hesitated a moment, cleared his throat and looked down at the floor.

She grabbed his arm and pleaded, "I have to know!"

"Lisl," he began hoarsely, "parts of *Frau* Meiers's body, two little heads and a baby's arm are in a casket down at the funeral home."

"No! No! No!" she screamed as bitter tears spilled down her face washing away the sand and the mud.

"Oh, God, why couldn't You bless them and keep them well? Why?"

Herr Kohler's eyes welled with tears, as he held the girl close and comforted her, her body racking with sobs. Lisl cried herself out as he gently told her that *Frau* and *Herr* Weber's bodies were never even found. The pent-up tensions of the past few weeks, with the continuous bombings and constant runs to the bunker, were released that day as she sat in the hospital bed crying the grit and dirt out of her eyes. She felt totally forlorn and abandoned — having lost everything, including her home and her dearest friend. She realized then, at that horrible moment of truth, that nothing was safe; nothing was ever certain. In that one moment, the innocence of her youth was transformed into the aged wisdom that comes only from a lifetime of tears and sorrow. All she could think of was Altmannstein. She wanted to go home to her parents. She had no home in Regensburg any longer, and there was no reason for her to stay.

"*Herr* Kohler," Lisl said, heaving a weary sigh, "I want to go home."

Seeing the look of despair on her face, he promised to return for her just as soon as he could get a reserve director to fill in for him.

Although grimy and bloody from the many lacerations on her legs and arms, her most serious injuries were a concussion and a badly bruised rib cage. Every breath hurt and the slightest movements caused searing pain in her side. For the next few days while in the hospital, Lisl drifted in and out of medicated sleep. Her few moments of wakefulness were fraught with crashing despair. Her only hope now was *Herr* Kohler. Would he come back for her as he had promised? she thought. Everyone else that she had known in Regensburg was gone.

At night she lay awake in the dark ward listening to the soft moaning of the other patients around her. She replayed in her mind what *Herr* Kohler had told her, and fresh tears sprang to her eyes. Why was she one of the few to survive? she agonized. Why did Irene have to die? And her sweet little boys! Each heart-wrenching thought brought on a new avalanche of emotion — relief, anger, confusion, guilt. She searched for answers and understanding, but found none. Again Lisl kept coming back to the only thing left for her to do, and that was to go home to the parents that she prayed to God were still safe. Once home Lisl could only hope and pray that this war and all of its misery would soon end. She prayed to God for strength. The strength to go on.

The following week, true to his word, *Herr* Kohler appeared with a clean, dry dress for her to wear. In seeing *Herr* Kohler's familiar face, Lisl felt her strength and determination return. Like a torrential flood rushing over a dry, cracked river bottom, so had her new-found strength flowed through her body.

"Lisl," he said with a smile, "we're going home."

CHAPTER 5

Lisl leaned her head against the cool windowpane and felt the rhythmic vibrations of the train as it sped into the night. *Herr* Kohler was dozing in the seat next to her, his head bobbing on his chest. It was a miracle that they were even on the train, she thought, remembering the events of the day.

After leaving the hospital that cold, rainy morning, they had planned to take the streetcar to the train station three miles away. The two had not walked very far before realizing that the streetcar tracks had been completely destroyed. Lisl's heart sank as she stared at the derailed cars — their tracks lying before them like giant, broken match sticks.

"Are you up to a little hike?" *Herr* Kohler asked.

Lisl knew he was only trying to make light of the situation to keep her spirits up. "Of course," she replied, forcing a smile. Her only thoughts were of home. They trudged onward to the train station, their silence broken by the incessant sirens warning them of yet another bombing. Taking shelter briefly then continuing on again, they made their way through the bombed city. Regensburg no longer wore the genteel charm of a Renaissance city. Its historic buildings, their architecture once grand and noble, were now piles of useless stone, stucco and wood. As they passed the spot where the grand hotel, The Golden Swan, used to be, Lisl noticed its ornate wrought-iron sign squeaking mournfully in the wind as it lay on top of the rubble. At the sight of the pathetic sign, Lisl faltered. Her legs buckled, and she fell to her knees in front of the pile of stone that used to be The Golden Swan, a hotel once proud and rich in tradition. She felt as though her very foundation had been yanked from underneath her, and she started screaming. "What's to become of us, *Herr* Kohler?" she cried. "This building was a landmark! It had been here for hundreds of years and now look at it! Will they not stop until everything has been destroyed?" She covered her face with her hands and cried.

"Lisl… Lisl… my dear, you must be brave — you must be strong!" *Herr* Kohler was now pulling her to her feet.

"I can't! I can't anymore."

"Yes, you can. Now come, we've got to make that train. You want to see your Mama and Father again, don't you? You have to be a good little soldier."

Lisl took a deep breath to regain her composure, then continued to walk while holding onto the older man's arm.

All around them people were scurrying everywhere tending to the injured and the dying. Hunched-over workers carted off countless corpses, covering their bloated and stiff forms with sheets. As they passed one heavily loaded cart, the wind caught one corner of the sheet momentarily, and Lisl stared into the unseeing eyes of a young girl no more than sixteen years old. That could have been her! she realized with horror. If *Herr* Kohler hadn't been there to rescue her, she would have surely died and been carted away like some unwanted litter in the street. She clung fiercely to *Herr* Kohler's arm as she shuddered at her thoughts.

"Are you cold, Lisl?" *Herr* Kohler asked.

"No, I can make it," Lisl said feebly.

"Remember now, we all have to be good soldiers, you know," he repeated with a reassuring smile.

"I — I know. But it's just so hard," she said, her voice breaking.

What struck her as particularly traumatic were the smells: the acrid smell of smoke, the burning oil and gasoline, the vile stench of broken waste lines, the smell of bodies rapidly rotting in the streets — all mingled together in an evil conglomeration of death.

The smoke-streaked, fire-blistered walls of what were once pristine white buildings towered above them, their contents spilling out of large, gaping holes. In the street before them a blood-covered man lay crumpled and moaning. As they passed, his hand reached out for Lisl's foot, and she knelt to help him.

"No, Lisl, we don't have time! Let the ambulance get him," *Herr* Kohler urged as he pulled her away.

"But we should do something!" Lisl cried.

"What? What are we going to do!" *Herr* Kohler shouted as he held tight to her arm and pulled her along. "There are thousands like him and they're dying faster than we can help them. Our best chance is to get out of the city while we still can, or else *we'll* be lying in the street like that! Believe me, there was nothing we could do to help that man — he was too far gone."

Finally, they arrived at the station only to find out that their train had just departed. It would be the next day before they could catch another one. Heartbroken and dejected, Lisl could only wonder: how would they make it? We *will* make it, she told herself over and over. As *Herr* Kohler kept reminding her, she had to be a "good soldier" even though she was losing courage.

As thin columns of smoke rose all around them, they determined that the only shelter available to them for the night would be the train station, and so, their long wait began. As early morning light appeared outside the window, the train that would eventually take them to Altmannstein pulled in at the platform. With eyes gritty from fatigue, *Herr* Kohler and Lisl ran quickly to board as smoke and steam from the giant locomotive swirled around their feet. The relief Lisl felt as they found their seats was short-lived. The pair soon realized that what would have been a three-hour ride home became a perilous, exhausting two-day journey.

The cause of the countless delays was the cursed air raid sirens that forced the train to stop with each attack and allow the passengers to scatter into the nearby forest for shelter. Each time they stopped to obey the sirens and take cover in the woods, no one knew for sure if the train they had momentarily abandoned would survive the attack or be destroyed by an ill-timed bomb leaving them all stranded in the rural countryside. After each attack the weary, bedraggled passengers would return to the train once more, cold, sodden from the rain, but always ready to continue a little further.

The Allies' air offensives over Germany were certainly taking their toll. The deep green forests that were once the happy playground for a six-year old farm girl and her father now provided life-saving cover from the never-ending death and destruction that dropped continually from the skies.

Herr Kohler's labored breathing next to Lisl told her he was taking a severe cold. As for herself, she tried hard to ignore the nagging pain in her lower back and abdomen. She knew she had to be brave and hold back her emotions — at least for now.

A shiver ran down her spine as she caught her reflection in the window. A haunted young girl stared back at her — blue-green eyes filled with sorrow, pain and a profound grief beyond measure. The blood-covered face of the man lying in the gutter of Regensburg haunted her now. *Herr* Kohler's words echoed in her mind: "We can't help him now — he's too far gone." How many more would die before this horror would end? Would anything ever be the same again? She thought of The Golden Swan, that wonderful hotel now reduced to rubble. Lisl knew in her heart that, at least for her, the answer was a definite "no." The sunny innocence of her pre-war childhood seemed eons away — vague memories now — like some soft-focus dream scene of another era. She felt as though she had lived a thousand years already. Reluctantly, the young Lisl had been thrust into the calculated, adult sphere of a war she had no say in, and she silently mourned the loss of innocence for all of them.

Sleep was almost impossible now, and she braced herself at the shriek of the air raid sirens as once more the train rolled to a halt and the passengers headed for the forest again. The constant bone-chilling rain wore at even the hardiest of passengers. Brambles tearing at her legs, Lisl clung to *Herr* Kohler as they made their way back to the train for a final time.

At last, the darkness of night gave way to pink and gray fingers of dawn streaking the sky once more, and Lisl knew they were almost home. Home. The word itself brought tears to her eyes as she pictured her beloved mother, hands on her hips, standing at the gate of their house. The dull, throbbing pain in her lower abdomen had by now become a searing burn that was difficult to ignore. Her heart raced as she watched familiar landmarks come into view. It seemed like forever before the train lumbered into the station, and *Herr* Kohler and Lisl stepped down onto the platform. Their arduous journey together had come to an end, so the two decided to part ways at the station.

"I can't thank you enough, *Herr* Kohler, for everything you've done for me," Lisl said. "You saved my life and brought me home — and for that I'm eternally grateful to you!" She held his gnarled and trembling hands in hers.

With tears and kisses and a last hug, he said, "Take care of yourself, Lisl."

She watched as he ambled down the road that led to his house — his stooped frame racked with incessant coughing, and Lisl silently prayed that he would recover.

Suddenly, she was filled with a vague sense of urgency — as if she were missing out on something and had to get home right away. She felt like a child again. The aching fatigue from the long journey all but forgotten now, she headed in the direction of her house. Passing all the familiar places of her youth — the church, the restaurants, the bakery — she marveled at the calm, the natural order of everyday life here. If there was a small remnant of decency left in the world, surely it was here in this little rural town seemingly untouched by the ravages of war. How ironic to come from the burning destruction — bodies blown to bits and the ruins of a shattered city like Regensburg — to the quiet peacefulness of Altmannstein.

Here women were going about their morning chores: hanging down-filled comforters out bedroom windows to catch the morning breeze; in the streets housewives were carrying home their daily purchases in string net bags; old men sitting together in doorways, their pipe smoke circling their heads in wispy haloes; children, lots of children, playing hide-and-seek in flower gardens. Where did all these children come from? she wondered. Most of them were quite young and now living with the older residents of Altmannstein. What Lisl was to learn later was that when the bombings of the big cities began, many city dwellers quickly shipped their offsprings to friends and relatives who lived in the country where the children could live out of harm's way for the duration of the war. Apparently, the fresh country air agreed with these children as was evidenced by their rosy cheeks and happy, gleeful faces.

Lisl hastened her steps. The tranquil tableau before her could not calm the excitement she felt as she stumbled and ran up the hill that led to her parents' house.

"I'm home!" Lisl cried as her mother's arms enveloped her. She looked up into her mother's face and saw that Maria had been crying. "It's alright, Mama, I'm home."

"We were so worried… your father almost went mad when he heard of the heavy bombing in Regensburg. He hasn't been himself the last few days. He'll be so happy to see you. We had no way of knowing until we got the message from *Frau* Kohler… Oh, Lisl, I'm so glad you're alright!" Maria pressed her wet cheek against her daughter's hair. They stood together for a while. As she held Lisl's face in her hands, the relief on Maria's face at seeing her youngest child safe once again was quickly replaced with concern. She felt her feverish forehead. "You're ill! Let's get you upstairs and into bed. Go quickly now. I'll send for Dr. Singer," she said.

Exhausted, Lisl fell into bed. The ordeal of the past few days had extracted its price. The Wenzel's good friend and family physician, Dr. Singer, diagnosed Lisl as having a severe kidney infection and ordered extended bed rest. It seemed as if she slept for days. Between the prescribed medication, the bed rest, and the love of her family, however, she was soon on the road to recovery.

CHAPTER 6

Although no one knew for sure that the war was nearing its end, in the winter of 1944, life took on a far more treacherous aspect for the family. Word of frequent disappearances of Jews had reached the back corners of Bava n Altmannstein, the Hohensteins and Zieglers, had received their notice of a call up. They now knew they were in danger of being shipped off to prison. Up until now they had been among the lucky few to survive a roundup. Kindly neighbors had provided them with falsified papers, which together with their blonde, blue-eyed coloring kept both families out of the scrutiny of the authorities. Their first thoughts were to flee, but all travel for Jews was forbidden, and their time was running out.

Maria came downstairs to the living room one evening to see Michael, Peter Hohenstein and Theo Ziegler sitting at the table with their heads bent towards each other engrossed in quiet conversation.

"You realize, Michael, that this plan of yours would jeopardize your whole family — I'm not sure we want to do this to you. We've all been friends too long for us to deliberately endanger you like this," Peter said.

He leaned back, folded his arms and eyed his host affectionately. Michael Wenzel was the first Gentile in the community to befriend him six years ago when the Hohensteins first came to Altmannstein from Nürnberg. The Hohensteins had been forced to give up their thriving jewelry business, sell off many of the opulent furnishings from their home in Nürnberg, and move out into the country to escape the ever-tightening government restrictions that made it difficult, if not impossible, for a Jew to earn a living. Back in Nürnberg everywhere one went, the hated *JUDEN VERBOTEN* signs seemed to prevail. Once settled in Altmannstein, however, Peter had quietly opened a watch repair shop to bring in a little income. Their grown sons had long since left home, both emigrating to Palestine, but for Lillian and Peter, Germany was still their homeland no matter what kind of government was in power. Now, once again, it seemed he was running and hiding, this time calling on the goodness of his dear friend. He couldn't help but recall the many enjoyable Sunday afternoons spent playing cards with Michael Wenzel and their friends in the local tavern.

"What choice do we have, Peter?" Michael replied refilling their glasses from the pitcher of beer that stood in the center of the table. "If you don't stay with us, you will surely be in danger." Michael had heard the stories spoken in hushed tones of how government dissidents, Jews, Gypsies, anyone that the Nazis considered enemies of the Reich, were subjected to beatings, torture and starvation in the prison camps. His stomach turned at the thought of what the Nazis were doing, and now this was his chance to help fight this virulent hatred that was taking over his country. If he couldn't save them all, at least he could save his neighbors. It was the only decent thing to do, and, in his mind, there was no other option. "It's *because* we've been friends for so long that I insist you both allow us to do this," he said.

Maria heard the conviction in her husband's voice and stood behind his chair with her hands on his shoulders as an affirmation of his words. "Peter, we've been friends for so long," she said. "We've supplied your families with milk and butter for years. We can't let anything happen to you now. We can manage. If you stay quiet during the day, we will be able to do it. This is the only way to keep all of you safe, believe me."

"Then it's all set," Michael said as he placed both hands on the table, "I won't hear any more objections."

Theo Ziegler, the older of the two men listened quietly. He and his Sophie had not known the Wenzels as well as the Hohensteins, but were now, nevertheless, entrusting their lives to these people. It seemed hard to believe that this stern-looking farmer with the pale blue eyes would put his life and the lives of his family on the line for them. Theo, a short, stocky man had come from Berlin. His wife was of aristocratic stock and had been reluctant to move from the big city to such a small berg as Altmannstein. But things had been bad in Berlin in the '30s — friends disappeared into thin air, synagogues were burned, Jewish stores were looted. The Zieglers came to Altmannstein looking for a little peace. They wanted to be left alone. It didn't matter that there was no synagogue in the tiny berg. All Theo had wanted in life was to take care of his Sophie and provide for her. Now that their lives were in jeopardy once again, they were at the mercy of these humble farm people, the Wenzels. It was a strange hand that fate had dealt them all.

Peter and Theo exchanged rueful smiles, and their eyes filled with tears. "Thank you both," Theo said.

As Maria prepared for bed that night, she heard the three men work out the details. Presently, Michael came up to sit by her bedside. "I'm going over to their apartments and bring over some of their clothes and things — whatever household items I can carry. It would be better for me to get a few things from them than for both families to be seen carrying all their belongings to our house," he explained holding her hand.

"Oh, Michael, is that safe?" she worriedly asked.

"It's far safer for me to be seen with a burlap bag than for them to be seen with a suitcase."

"Please be careful! Don't let anyone see you."

"At this hour, there's no one on the street so it should be fairly safe." He kissed her quickly and called over his shoulder as he headed toward the door, "It may take me a while, so don't wait up."

The next evening, once again under the cover of dark the Zieglers and the Hohensteins arrived at the Wenzel's house with not only a few more personal belongings, but each family member wore several layers of clothing in preparation for a long wait. They had draped dust covers over their furniture and placed a sign that read "Gone To Switzerland" on their apartment door. As far as the townspeople knew, the two Jewish families had vanished into thin air. While Lisl was living in Regensburg at the time, the two couples were to hide out in her bedroom until the SS moved out of the area, and it was safe for everyone. Once Lisl came back from Regensburg, they then moved further upstairs to the now-unused smokehouse. None of them had any idea how long it would last, but the Wenzels were prepared to continue to protect the Jewish families for the duration of the war, if necessary.

The Wenzels' house was built into the side of a mountain, and the smokehouse occupied part of the attic. It was accessible two ways: one, through a small door leading out onto the craggy face of the mountain with only a narrow path leading up to it; the other was a trap door in the floor that led down to one of the bedrooms on the second floor. Michael installed an electrical outlet in the smokehouse so that the families could listen to the news on their small short-wave radio. Once the two couples were settled in their new quarters, it became Lisl's job to bring them food at night. This was no easy accomplishment as the Wenzels had only three ration cards from which to draw. They no longer had the farm or the livestock to go with it, and so it became a daily challenge for Maria to make their meager rations stretch to feed four more people. Somehow through it all, she always managed. The smokehouse had, of course, no toilet facilities or wash area. Although she was still recuperating from her illness after the ordeal in Regensburg, Lisl not only brought the families their food basket each night, but also a fresh pitcher of water and an enamelware basin. Each morning she then lowered the ladder to the trap door and took down the water buckets containing their wastes. They dared not run to the privy, even late at night, for fear of being spotted by a neighbor. No, the Hohensteins and Zieglers had to remain in total secrecy not just for their sake, but for the sake of the Wenzel family, as well.

"Mama, why do we bring meals to our friends upstairs only late at night?" Lisl asked one evening in late March as she and her mother were preparing their food basket. Maria had cooked a vegetable stew from the day's meager garden harvest and was tucking in a few slices of rye bread.

"They sleep in the daytime, Lisl, so they won't make any noise that might be heard by someone outside or possibly the neighbors — we can't trust anyone to know about them. Things are so uncertain nowadays, you just don't know who to trust anymore," she said sadly shaking her head.

Lisl's mouth went dry with the thought of what might happen to her family as well as their friends in the smokehouse. The Hohensteins and the Zieglers had not even been in hiding three months and already there had been idle inquiries by neighbors. Fritz Krueger, more pompous and officious than ever, had asked her father, supposedly in passing conversation, if he, Michael, had any idea where the Zieglers or the Hohensteins might have disappeared to. It was now a well-known fact that *Herr* Krueger was in agreement with the dictatorial government and was considered a spy working for the feared and dreaded secret police. He represented the Party at the local level, having been assigned to a low-level clerical post that Krueger interpreted into something far more that intended. On more than one occasion, a long black Nazi staff car was seen parked at the Krueger's home late at night.

Both Michael and Maria had to be extremely careful with the information they had. Even Lisl's older sister in Munich had no idea that her family was protecting Jewish neighbors in their house.

As Lisl carried the food-laden basket to the attic, she recalled how she used to bring buttermilk to the women who now occupied this attic.

"Lisl!" Lillian whispered with a smile. There was a fresh sparkle in her eyes as she helped open the trapdoor. "We just heard on the radio that the Allies have crossed the Rhine! The American Army crossed over on March 7, at Remagen," she explained excitedly. They had been listening to the BBC on the short-wave. "It won't be long now and we'll all be free." Her husband crouched on the floor in front of the tiny radio and continued to adjust the dials while cocking his ear toward the speaker. Sophie looked up from the book she was holding and smiled her greeting at Lisl, then continued to read while her husband Theo took the heavy basket from the girl.

"That would mean the end of all the fighting, wouldn't it?" Lisl asked. "And then we could go on with our lives like before all this madness began."

"From your mouth to God's ear!" Peter Hohenstein said wistfully.

Lisl sat down on a footstool in front of the low table where Lillian began dividing up the food for the four of them. "You know, I remember how happy you always were when Mama put a dollop of butter in the buttermilk I delivered to you every Friday," Lisl said. "You knew Mama would put the butter in, yet you were always so surprised and happy when you discovered it there."

"Yes, well — it was always such a generous gesture, I guess I was just so grateful for it. And remember how before you left, we would go down to our root cellar, and I'd give you a handful of carrots? My, how you loved carrots! I would tell Peter when he came home, 'The way that Lisl Wenzel loves carrots, she's going to turn completely orange someday!' That's what I would tell him," Lillian replied pointing her butter knife at Peter while she talked.

They all chuckled at the memories. Lisl looked around at the four adults in the room and thought fleetingly of how pale-white they'd become in the short few months of hiding. Their eyes had permanent dark circles under them, and their features were becoming slightly drawn from the constant tension and worry. She wished she could do more to cheer them with her visits and break up the agonizing monotony of their day. "Well, it won't be long now — let's all hope," she said as she stood up and picked up the empty basket. "See you tomorrow." She waved as she eased herself down the steep ladder.

One day, as Maria stood in line at the meat market, she overheard two women comment on the mysterious disappearance of the two Jewish families. It was obvious from the conversation that the townspeople assumed the two families had been picked up by the Gestapo and possibly sent to prison. Maria wanted desperately to reassure these people that the Hohensteins and the Zieglers were safe. If only she could confide in these women and let them know their neighbors were alive! Yet, no one really knew these days... oh, what unsure times they were all living in. Neighbors distrustful of neighbors. Friends suspicious of friends. These were women she had known for twenty years — they had shared so much. What was the matter with her? Why couldn't she tell these people that their friends were okay? Would things ever be the same again? She knew that the ways of war were always the same. It had happened to her country once before, and she had lived through it. Now she must endure it again. When war comes to your village — your own doorstep, you do what you must. In the end she realized that she simply could not confide in anyone. Prudence kept her silent: informers were everywhere, and she knew that to tell anyone of the families' whereabouts would surely jeopardize everyone involved.

It seemed the Zieglers and Hohensteins had not been with the Wenzels very long when they heard from neighbors that the SS officers were in Altmannstein, and a thorough search of all homes was being conducted to flush out anybody who had not answered their draft call. The word was also that any citizen found guilty of hiding Jews would be rounded up and sent to labor camps and prisons along with the Jews.

One rainy evening as Lisl sat knitting on the living room sofa, there was a loud knock at the door. Maria looked up from her sewing with a terrified expression on her face. Michael silently motioned for the two of them to continue their work while he slowly opened the front door and invited the two officers standing there to come in.

"Gentlemen, come in, come in. It's cold out there. Can we offer you something to eat or drink?" Michael sounded far more amicable than he felt as he allowed the two officers in.

"Thank you — no, we are here on official business. The *Hauptsturmführer* over this area has word of some Jews who have not answered their draft notices, and we were told that you might be able to help us find them," replied one of the officers.

"Now, why would *I* have any information about any Jews? I don't even know the *Hauptsturmführer,*" Michael said returning the officer's steady gaze.

"Perhaps not, *Herr* Wenzel," the officer maintained his courteous manner. "However, *Herr* Krueger thought…"

"*Herr* Krueger? Fritz Krueger does not know my business! He has asked me repeatedly if I have any information, and I'll tell you the same thing that I told Fritz. I don't know of any Jews that have not answered their draft notices."

Lisl's heartbeat quickened as she listened carefully to the officers articulate their orders to take these Jews, once they find them, into custody, and a sudden chill came over her.

"No... no. I will tell you again: no Jews have even been seen here in quite some time," Michael said stroking his chin as if searching his memory. "I will tell you this — I've heard that some may have fled to Switzerland."

"Yes, that is rumored, although unlikely. May I remind you, *Herr* Wenzel, if you are found lying, you too will go to prison," the shorter of the two officers said, his cold eyes fixed on Michael.

Michael remained steadfastly unperturbed. "I cannot tell you what I don't know," he replied with a shrug.

The two men that stood in the middle of the living room looked identically intimidating. Tall and blonde, they each wore the full-cut black uniform of the SS Guard, the corp d'elite of the Nazi Party — high-peaked cap, double-breasted jacket over black trousers, jack boots that glistened from the rain and a large square-shouldered overcoat cinched in at the waist with a wide belt. On their left arm they each wore the crimson band with the black swastika on it. Lisl surreptitiously studied them. Their manner was ever-polite and deferential to her father, but underneath the impersonal smiles, she saw a cold, calculated hardness. The shorter of the two had sky-blue eyes rimmed with thick, blonde lashes. He was obviously the younger one, and it was apparent that he was less experienced than the older officer. Imposing and officious, they stood conferring together while silently dripping rain on the floor.

Lisl fervently prayed that no noises would come from the smokehouse. Her heart pounded so fiercely in her chest, she thought surely the whole world would hear it. After an interminable silence broken by crashing thunder and the hissing rain, one of the men finally said to the other, "Let's go, there's nothing here."

The two men abruptly left, and as Michael closed the door behind them, he leaned against it and drew a ragged breath.

Maria ran to him with relief and said, her voice barely above a whisper, "I was so afraid that they would take all of us!"

"You and Lisl did just fine, Mama," he said giving her a hug.

A few days later the Wenzels learned that the SS had moved on, and the Hohensteins and Zieglers lived out the remaining few months of the war in the smokehouse. Subsequently that following spring when the victorious Allies marched into Altmannstein on that jubilant day in May of 1945, the local citizenry and the Wenzels had more than one reason to celebrate the end of the war: the survival of the Hohenstein and Ziegler families as well.

Lisl realized many years later what the Wenzel family had done by sheltering the two Jewish couples during those last few months of the war was not a conscious act of bravery or heroism. It was, in fact, an act of humanity carried out by many families throughout the continent. It was what needed to be done at the time to save friends and loved ones. Because of the compassion and decency of thousands of self-appointed protectors, Lisl was to learn, hundreds of thousands of Jews were either smuggled to safety or kept hidden and alive. Certainly there were the well-known heroes such as the protectors of Anne Frank, whose diary first drew the world's attention to the plight of Jews in Nazi Germany, or the famous German businessman, Oskar Schindler, who recruited twelve hundred Jews as essential war workers for his enamelware factory to save them from the death camps. One seldom read, however, of these little known acts of courage performed by ordinary people for, as in any war, it is the victor that writes the history and, consequently, these unsung heroes fade into obscurity. And yes, Lisl thought, among the bravest of these unsung heroes were Germans, themselves, for they performed their acts of mercy under the very noses of the Gestapo. As Lisl was to discover years later, documented cases abounded of Germans such as Dr. Franz Kauffmann of Berlin who routinely hid Jews and established an intricate network of friends who kept the Jewish fugitives constantly on the move, and consequently avoided discovery. Lisl even read of a German officer, Anton Schmidt, stationed in Poland, who had hidden and protected Jews in the basement of three residences that were under his command and were the official property of the German Army.

The Anti-Semitism of Nazi Germany that one reads about in history books had not made itself felt in the backlands of Bavaria — at least, not in Altmannstein. Neighbor still helped neighbor. In fact, neighbor depended on neighbor. In the rural community of Altmannstein, as in rural communities since time immemorial, hardships such as illness or death of a loved one were eased when shared with loving and concerned neighbors. Harvesting of crops was shared, and when the need was there, differences of religious beliefs were never part of the equation.

Until the war would be over, life went on quietly and as normally as possible for the rural citizens of Altmannstein. With an ever-watchful eye on the uncertain future, parents did what they could to raise responsible children, keep their families intact, and, most of all — above all — survive. And so, at least for the Wenzel family, in spite of the senseless madness of World War II in Germany, life had to go on.

"It's good to see a bloom in your cheeks again, Lisl," Maria smiled as she handed her daughter a cup of hot tea. The fragrant peppermint warmed Lisl's stomach as she slowly sipped the golden brew.

"*Was dich nicht umbringt, macht dich stärker*" — what didn't kill you made you stronger," she said with a chuckle quoting Nietzsche, the great German philosopher. Lisl had been nursed back into walking condition and was now resting on the bench in her mother's flower garden, where the thin sunshine of an early spring shone down on her frail body. Maria hesitated briefly before she reached into the pocket of her apron and pulled out an official-looking envelope.

"This came for you in the mail this morning," she added averting her eyes to hide the concern.

Lisl swung her legs to the ground and tore open the letter to read what was basically her official draft notice. Her stomach lurched as she realized she was to report to work the following Monday at a munitions factory in Desching, thirty kilometers away. Her father had already been drafted to work there and now it seemed, she, too, was destined to do her part for the war effort — in spite of her age, her physical condition or her political beliefs. Dr. Singer has already written numerous letters to the state employment agency explaining that the girl was too ill to work. Apparently, it was all in vain — for the next day, a state inspector appeared at their door.

"I am here to make sure your daughter will be reporting for duty," he said coldly.

"But she is still ill. Our doctor has already sent a letter to the officials," Maria protested.

The uniformed officer brusquely strode past her mother to where Lisl was lying on the couch.

"*Fräulein* Wenzel, you must do your part for your country, the Fatherland. If you resist, you may wind up in prison," he said.

"Then I'll just go to prison," Lisl retorted with a defiant lift of her chin.

His face drained of all color and his voice took on an ominous tone as he leaned toward her, his face close to hers and said, "No, no, *Fräulein* Wenzel, you do not ever want that to happen. The prison you'd go to is Dachau, near Munich, and, believe me, you don't want to go there!"

None of them at the time, of course, had any idea what he was alluding to and, in the end, it was her wise mother who assured him that they would make the appropriate arrangements so that Lisl could report to work as required.

"She will be there Monday morning at eight a.m.," Maria said as she escorted the official to the door.

"Make sure that she does!" With a curt nod and a click of his heels, he turned and was gone.

Presently Lisl realized she had no choice — that she was being pressed into service against her will. She resigned herself to make the best of it. But, first, there was one more thing she had to do.

That Sunday afternoon, she decided to go down to the little town cemetery to visit Stefan's grave one more time. Trudi's brother's remains had been found and shipped back to Altmannstein a few weeks after his tragic death. Stopping first at a flower shop to buy a small bouquet, Lisl hurried down the cobblestone street alone. It had been a cold, wet winter and now that spring was here, the leaded sky promised even more rain and high winds. As she slowly opened the creaking gate to the cemetery, Lisl noticed how many newly-dug graves had been added to the hallowed patch of land. The air smelled dank and earthy from the freshly turned dark mounds. The war was taking all the young men Altmannstein had to offer and quickly filling up its cemetery with their remains. The wind howled in the trees and a lone crow cried mournfully in the sky. Lisl pulled her billowing coat tighter around her skirt and shivered as she read the words on the granite headstone: "Stefan Heinrich Hofer, beloved son and brother. Born: February 2, 1925. Died In Service To His Country: December 13, 1943." Lisl sank to her knees in front of the grave as tears spilled down her face and splashed on the grave's granite border. Oh, Stefan, she thought: Why did you have to die? She placed the flowers tenderly in a brass urn at the foot of the grave and sprinkled holy water on it from a small container in the corner of the little plot. After a short while, she crossed herself, then slowly turned to head back home.

Michael rode his motorcycle to work each Monday, stayed overnight in the barracks during the week, then came back home again on Saturdays. Gasoline rations were two liters a week for them, so Lisl knew she would have to stay at the factory during the week also.

As Michael's motorcycle had no passenger seat, he fashioned one for his daughter with a sofa pillow secured to the back with a string. There were also no foot rests for a passenger, making it necessary for the girl to ride in the back with her feet held precariously out to the sides.

Finally, Monday morning arrived and father and daughter prepared for their first trip to the munitions plant together. The smell of rain was in the air as they stood outside the house. Westward, the clouds were darkening with an approaching storm, but to the east, the sky was streaked with the gold and lavender that heralded the morning sun.

Her face still pale and drawn from her recent illness, Lisl climbed onto the motorcycle and held tightly to Michael's waist as she wondered what was in store for her. As Michael revved up the motorcycle, Lisl turned her head to watch her mother waving good-bye with one hand and wiping her eyes with the other. Over the roar of the machine, Lisl shouted, "We'll be home soon. I love you!"

Lisl felt lucky to be able to ride to work with her father, and whatever they encountered they could deal with together. At least, she wouldn't be alone. However, it did seem grossly unfair. She was a civilian, for heaven's sake. How could they ask her to do this? To be drafted into civil service at her age was preposterous. Fortunately, her father seemed to think the end was drawing near. In spite of the valiant attempts of the media to continue to paint a rosy picture on behalf of the Fatherland, Michael suspected that Germany was now losing more battles than it was winning. Rumors of retreating troops were becoming more rampant every day. Hopefully, she would not have to do whatever work was thrust upon her for very long.

As they approached the gates of the plant, the brown uniformed guard sauntered out to inspect the new arrival. "Halt! Please identify the young lady," he demanded.

"Just a new hire reporting in," Michael answered, his voice totally void of emotion.

"I must see her *Kennkarte*," the young guard demanded.

"She doesn't have one yet. Today is her first day here," Michael replied evenly.

Hesitating only briefly, the guard raised the crossbars, and they made their way to the front office. Lisl dropped off her coat at the women's barracks and then proceeded to the registration office to report in.

Orientation was swift and non-eventful as a pleasant-looking woman gave her a map of the plant and helped her with her identification card. Once orientation was completed, she was led through a maze of buildings and hallways to a large, high-ceilinged chamber. Typewriters clacked in an incessant staccato, telephones rang, and black-uniformed men scurried about as Lisl followed the woman into a small inner office to meet her new supervisor.

Bernard Holzbauer looked up from his paperwork to greet the

new arrival. "Good morning. And you are?" he asked.

"Lisl — Lisl Wenzel," she said timidly.

Holzbauer removed his glasses wearily, leaned back in his chair and rubbed the bridge of his nose. "Have you any experience in factory work, *Fräulein* Wenzel?"

"None at all, *Herr* Holzbauer," was the reply.

"Very well then, you will have to be a quick student. Learn everything you can and as quickly as you can. We have no time for mistakes. We are running at full production with round the clock shifts. Everyone pulls his or her load one hundred percent. Do you understand what I am saying?"

"Certainly, *Herr* Holzbauer," Lisl answered.

The pale green eyes gazed at her steadily. Bernard was not unpleasant-looking for a man of his age. Although he was no longer trim, Lisl guessed him to be in his early fifties. His blonde hair was closely-cropped giving him a boyish appeal. The startling pale eyes stared back at her from a face fleshy and strong-featured.

"If there are no questions," he said as he rose from his chair, "then follow me."

"Where — where am I going?" Lisl stammered in confusion as she followed him down a long corridor.

"To work!" he boomed, his voice echoing in the vast hallway.

Slightly dazed, Lisl looked around in fascination as people everywhere were engrossed in their tasks — tedious, repetitive assembly line motions combined in a strange cadence with the ceaseless chatter of machines. The supervisor handed her a gas mask and showed her how to put it on. She soon learned that they were manufacturing tear gas — apparently with white onions. The acrid odor assaulted her nose and burned her eyes continually. On that first day, she awkwardly strapped the gas mask to her face and instantly felt violent waves of nausea overcome her. The claustrophobic panic that she felt from the hot, confining apparatus made her miserable. She ran to the bathroom several times that day, each time unable to stop the convulsive retching. Eventually, she was forced to go to her supervisor for help.

"Sir," she asked timidly as she stood before him in his office, "could I please work somewhere else? The gas mask is making me ill, and I cannot perform my duties properly."

He leaned back in his chair and stared at her. He made no attempt to hide the leer on his face as he eyed her breasts. Lisl's cheeks burned with anger and humiliation as she lowered her eyes to the floor.

"You've been here exactly three days, and you have the nerve to ask for a transfer already? You *are* a cheeky one, aren't you?" he asked languidly.

"Please, Sir, I'm thinking only of my work. I cannot be efficient if I'm ill all the time."

"Very well, then," he said abruptly, "I'll see what I can do." He picked up the phone and dialed a number.

"The new hire with the big breasts wants to transfer," he laughed.

Silent tears coursed down her cheeks as she listened to him share a crude joke with the other party. Soon, however, she was on her way again — this time to the hand grenade department.

Her job there was to sew little sacks together, which the man next to her, a French prisoner of war, then had to fill with powder. Although still a distasteful job, it was a vast improvement over the tear gas department and, as an added bonus, she was with people her own age for a change.

The prisoner of war was a stunningly handsome young man who had apparently been captured near Mannheim. Jean-Pierre Tambreau's pencil-thin mustache gave him a sophisticated air that Lisl found intriguing. With his tall frame, piercing blue eyes, and cleft chin, Jean-Pierre had a polished look about him that made women stare in his direction a little longer than good manners allowed. On her first day in the department, Lisl shyly gazed at him in secret admiration. He cast a fleeting smile her way in a silent welcome.

"Father," Lisl ventured one Saturday evening at the dinner table, "there is an attractive, young Frenchman that works next to me now, and I'd like to get to know him better since he *is* close to my age."

Michael's face clouded with worry. "I know the one you're talking about. He's a P.O.W., and you're better off keeping to yourself. As nice a young man as he might be, you would be fraternizing with the enemy, Lisl, if you became friendly with him. I've seen girls disappear for just talking with prisoners. Please, promise me you won't talk to him."

Lisl soon learned that while on the job they were not to talk openly at all to *any* of their co-workers. Thus, like all the other workers drafted to the munitions factory, she carried out her tasks in relative quiet.

Life at the factory was regimented and excruciatingly mundane. The women's barracks were always meticulously maintained and in topnotch shape. The floor was so spotless that one could eat off it only because the women were ordered to keep it that way. Lisl and her fellow draftees lived with a myriad of rules and regulations that no one dared to challenge. The food in the canteen, although meager, was passable. Often, Lisl would forgo the meal there to be with her father who frequently ate in his barracks.

Friendships were made in secret and thus, became more cherished. Long after the lights out call was made, whispered giggling could occasionally be heard in the darkness of the barracks as female workers indulged in the girlish gossip and the camaraderie that would have been part of their life in normal times.

The days passed without incident until one Monday, as Lisl and Michael rode their motorcycle back to work, they spotted a small, Allied reconnaissance airplane circling overhead. Later that night, after all the women in the barracks were in bed, she lay on her cot staring up at the blackness and wondered what the little airplane was all about. She knew that the munitions factory could be a prime bombing target for the Allies. It was situated deep in the pine forest with container-grown pine trees covering its flat roof for camouflage. How long before it would be discovered was anyone's guess, and Lisl wondered if she could survive another major bombing. With tears streaming from the corners of her eyes, she prayed fervently to God that the war would end soon. How much longer would it go on? Was the world going mad? Physically and emotionally exhausted, Lisl felt sure she could not bear this burden any longer.

Just then a flicker of light shone from outside her window. She sat upright in her bed and waited until it appeared again. This time a definite beam of light danced off the ceiling. Lisl quickly tiptoed to the window not wanting to disturb the others and saw her father standing outside her window holding a small flashlight. Alarmed, she hurried outside in her nightgown to see what was wrong.

"Be here and ready to leave for good tomorrow at five p.m. The war is almost over," he whispered. He gave her a quick hug and then disappeared into the darkness. She tiptoed back inside, her heart pounding with excitement. She realized her father was taking a calculated risk by leaving the munitions factory on his hunch that the end of the war was at hand, and that the authorities would soon be too busy retreating to come after them. But, Lisl knew, too, that having served in the first World War, her father could accurately interpret all the signs of the impending defeat. To think that all the fighting and bombing would soon be over — Lisl dared not rejoice in the knowledge and allow herself the luxury of contemplating what life would be like again. Defeat or victory — how could one foresee the outcome of events? Oh, but it mattered not. Not at this point. No, Lisl thought, what mattered now was peace. The peace that was soon at hand. She prayed that her father was right.

The next morning she could hardly concentrate on her tasks at hand for wondering what the evening would bring. The only friendship she had dared to risk was with a young refugee from Berlin named Helga. A waif of a girl, Helga somehow made her way to Desching to find work and survive after her parents and siblings had all been killed in one of the major bombings in Berlin. Helga was a strikingly beautiful girl with a massive mane of blonde hair that tumbled past her shoulders. Quiet and shy, she was much like Lisl — alone and afraid, and, therefore, welcomed the opportunity to share girlish concerns with someone her age. That day, Helga was waiting for her in the lunchroom.

"Lisl, what's wrong? You have some news, don't you," she asked, her eyes dancing with excitement.

"Here," Lisl said, handing the girl her home address, "the war is almost over, I'm certain." They clasped hands as Lisl gently explained her father's plans.

"How can you leave me here?" she cried. "I have no one else. What's to become of me?"

"Helga, everything will be all right. You will survive, I just know it," said Lisl as she thought of another dear friend who didn't survive in Regensburg.

"Please, please come to Altmannstein as soon as you can," she added. "Everything will turn out fine soon. I promise."

Before leaving that day, Lisl took perhaps the biggest risk to her safety. She tucked a note in one of the little sacks she had sewn and passed it on to the handsome Frenchman. The note told him that within twenty-four hours he would be a free man and that she simply wanted to say "good-bye" to him. After quickly reading her clandestine note, the Frenchman regarded her with a quizzical look. Lisl smiled back knowingly. From then on, his eyes sparkled with excitement, and neither one of them could keep a smile from their faces.

That afternoon, knowing that their time together in the munitions factory was drawing to an end, Lisl became even bolder than before and wrote Jean-Pierre another note. She wanted to let him know how much she thought of him and how she hoped they could continue to be friends after this terrible war was over. Perhaps it was a schoolgirl's crush or just the exhilarating feeling of knowing that freedom from the terror of this work was at hand, but Lisl never knew what possessed her to write the note that almost became her downfall. As she walked down the assembly aisle toward Jean-Pierre to deliver the note, *Herr* Holzbauer, her former supervisor from the tear gas department, suddenly stepped in front of her.

"What's going on here? Why aren't you at your workstation, *Fräulein* Lisl?" he asked.

"I — I was going to see Helga. I need to give her my address," she stammered.

"You do that, little girl," he snapped menacingly, "and I want to see you in my office on your next break, is that understood?"

"Yes — yes, *Herr* Holzbauer," she answered and quickly walked towards Helga's workstation.

"What was that all about?" Helga asked as Lisl came over to where her friend was waiting. "Lisl, are you in trouble?"

"I'm not only in trouble, but I disobeyed my father as well," Lisl said fighting back the tears.

"Let's go to the ladies' room, and you can tell me what happened," she said.

Once in the rest room, Lisl explained to Helga about the innocent note to Jean-Pierre, and how she would need to explain herself in the supervisor's office that afternoon.

"Just stay calm," she said, "everything will be alright. You didn't do anything wrong. They won't incarcerate you now. Surely they know the end is at hand. All one has to do is read the papers. Ever since the Allies crossed the Rhine, surely the authorities know it's a hopeless cause."

"Helga! You could be incarcerated for just saying that. What you're saying is treason!" Lisl exclaimed. "*They* don't think it's a hopeless cause, and, if they do, they certainly won't openly give up — these people that are running this war will never admit defeat!"

"Well, nevertheless, let's just both be strong and hold out a little longer so that we both can get out of this godforsaken place."

The afternoon break came and Lisl found herself knocking on the supervisor's door.

"*Herein,*" he said.

As she timidly opened the door, the supervisor rose from his chair and gestured for her to take a seat.

"Sit down, sit down, *Fräulein* Lisl," he offered with a pleasant smile.

As she sat down in one of the chairs across the desk from him, he studied her with a relaxed calm.

"You have a lovely face — so Aryan in feature! You are really quite beautiful, you know."

"*Danke, mein Herr,*" Lisl heard her voice falter. The idea of sitting here making small talk with this tall, stern-looking man filled her with apprehension and dread. She fought to breathe slowly and tried to ignore her lurching stomach. He rose to his feet slowly and came to stand within inches of where she was sitting.

As his index finger lightly traced the line of her jaw, he asked, "What was in the note you were taking to the Frenchman this morning?"

"Oh Sir, you misunderstand," she protested, "I wasn't taking it to the Frenchman. I told you I was simply giving Helga my address. I want her to visit me some weekend. That's all." Lisl hoped he wouldn't see the fine droplets of perspiration that she felt on her upper lip. The clock on the wall ticked interminably. He appeared to delight in Lisl's discomfiture.

"Giving Helga your address, were you?" he said, his voice softening to barely a whisper.

She nodded her head hoping he would sit back down. Instead he leaned toward her even further and said, "Perhaps you'll bring a note to *me* with your address on it so that I can spend a weekend with you sometime." He smiled revealing the gleam of two large, gold teeth.

His face loomed above her and she tried not to meet his gaze. Gone was the boyish-appeal from their first meeting. Now Bernard Holzbauer appeared menacingly evil. How like a predator bird his face seemed, Lisl thought — beaked nose, eyes bright and unblinking. Yet somehow years of excess had taken their toll in the sagging contours and the eyes sunk in puffs of flesh.

Lisl glanced at the gold wedding band on his finger and said, "But, Sir, you're a married man. I'm sure you have a wife to spend your weekends with." She knew that if she could banter somewhat with this man and perhaps cajole him into letting her go back to her work, she would escape the danger of whatever penalty was handed down for fraternizing with the enemy.

"Oh, this?" he said glancing at his wedding band, "this is just for the record. My wife is used to my not coming home for the weekend. She goes her way pretty much, and I go mine. Ours is merely a marriage of convenience. So how about it, my dear? If your house is not convenient, we can always go to my apartment — I keep a place in Garmisch where we could relax."

Lisl looked around the room as if to find some response to his question — the gray metal desk, the reams of papers stacked neatly all around, the book shelves that lined the far wall. Alas, the room offered no clue. Lisl's eyes fell on the loaded Luger lying on a table to the side of the desk.

"I'm not sure I really know you well enough," Lisl demurred. "If you give me a couple of days to think about it, I promise I'll give you an answer soon." She smiled as pleasantly as she could, all the while thinking how outrageous this whole thing was! Was he trying to intimidate her with the gun? If she could just buy her time, surely she and her father would be out of there permanently.

"You realize, of course, *Fräulein* Lisl, that this little matter between us is strictly confidential. We wouldn't want word of this to get out to the others, now would we?" he said pleasantly.

"Of course not, I understand perfectly," Lisl answered. Wanting to get out of there as fast as possible, she stood up from her chair and forced herself to walk as calmly as possible toward the door. Like a gentleman, he rushed to open the door for her, all the while smiling and shaking her hand. "I'll be waiting for your answer and hope we'll see each other soon," he whispered.

As she reached for the doorknob, he lifted her chin with his hand and bent down to kiss her — at first softly then suddenly harder and more urgently.

"No... please... no, *Herr* Holzbauer, no... please don't." Lisl fought the revulsion that churned in her stomach.

"Ah, you're so beautiful, Lisl — so very beautiful, I just can't help myself." He had her pinned against the door blocking her exit with one arm while groping under her blouse with the other. "I could make you so happy. You have no idea how happy I could make you. If you were mine, I'd shower you with jewels — you'd have everything you could ever want," he muttered as he continued to press his body up against her and smear her face with wet kisses.

"Please, *Herr* Holzbauer, I beg you...please stop!" Lisl felt as if she were gagging.

Suddenly he pulled back brushing his mouth with the back of his hand while he eyed her. "I mustn't frighten you." He smiled hideously. "I apologize, *Fräulein* Lisl. I will wait like a good boy for your answer," he said softly. "I hope we'll be together soon."

Not if I can help it, she thought grimly as she slipped out the door. As she walked passed Helga and Jean-Pierre, she shakily gave them both a circled thumb and index finger signal that all was okay. She then ran for the bathroom as her stomach began heaving violently. After a while, she stared at herself in the mirror. Her face was blotchy and swollen. I've got to pull myself together and not let him get to me, she reasoned. She could hardly wait for her shift to be over so she could go to the barracks and wait for her father to pick her up.

That evening father and daughter rendezvoused like clockwork at the corner of the women's barracks. As Lisl climbed onto his waiting motorcycle, Michael warned, "Now when we get to the gate, just hold on to me and let me do all the talking."

Approaching the gate they spotted the guard talking on the phone. Relief washed over Lisl as he motioned them to go on. She hung on to her father's waist for dear life as they sped toward home in the gathering darkness.

As they reached the outskirts of Altmannstein, they came upon a roadblock manned by two SS officers. Michael quickly turned his head back toward Lisl and hissed, "Lay your head on my back!" Needing no further explanation, she lay her head on his back, closed her eyes and groaned softly as they approached the SS officers.

"What have we here?" one asked. "Where are your papers?"

"I'm taking my daughter to the doctor — she is very ill," Michael explained.

"We will need to confiscate your motorcycle for official business, Sir," they replied.

"Yes, yes, of course," said Michael agreeably, "but first, let me take her to the doctor," throwing his head back in her direction. The officers conferred with each other out of earshot, and after a few tense moments, agreed to let them pass.

Once home, Maria met them with more distressing news: it appeared German foot soldiers faced with imminent defeat were taking civilian vehicles for escape. Several of the neighbors had had their bicycles, motorcycles and anything with wheels taken away from them. Apparently with its battle lines now severely broken, the German army was retreating rapidly in the face of the advancing Allies, and deserters were quite commonplace.

"Quick, Lisl, get the shovels and come with me," Michael ordered quietly.

Lisl wasn't sure what he had planned, but Lisl knew whatever he was thinking, it would be the right thing to do. The girl duly followed him to the back of the house.

"Help me dig a hole over there," he said pointing to a small clearing.

Their house had been built into the side of a mountain, so they had no real backyard to speak of. However, a gentle slope of the mountain side provided a small level patch of land. It was here where, as a younger child, Lisl had often played in the sun-dappled grass. Now she obediently followed her father's instruction, and the two of them began digging a deep hole. Quickly he set about the task of dismantling the motorcycle. One by one, they carefully laid each piece in the hole, then covered it all with the soft, rich soil. As they walked back to the house to wash their hands, Lisl glanced back and was amazed at their handiwork — he clearing looked almost untouched.

Earlier they had seen small groups of white tents with a bold red cross emblazoned on them situated on the hillsides. Michael immediately recognized this as a ruse. It was the SS officers retreating from the cities under the guise of the Red Cross as the Allies relentlessly advanced. That evening, as the three of them waited, they half-expected the SS officers that patrolled their town to come to their door searching for vehicles. Surprisingly, no one came. The air took on an eerie calm as the townspeople locked their doors, shuttered their windows, and waited. Michael and Lisl stood outside under the evening sky for a moment gazing at the other side of the valley.

Taking a puff from his pipe, he remarked, "It won't be long now."

Lisl looked up at him and saw blazing orange-red lights reflected in his eyes. Her eyes followed his gaze and she, too, stared at the brilliant red fire in the clouds. Across the valley the sky glowed smoky and crimson.

"You're looking at history being made, Lisl, for it won't be long before the Allies will be here. I can only pray that it will be a peaceful conclusion to this terrible war."

CHAPTER 7

Michael was uncannily accurate in his prediction, for the very next morning the town awoke to a half mile line of Allied tanks and troops poised on the hillside overlooking the valley.

"Maria, bring me a white tablecloth — the bigger, the better!" Michael suddenly commanded.

Maria complied, and with the help of an old broomstick, Michael fashioned a large white flag to hang from the second-story window as a silent signal to the advancing victor that they harbored no hostility and wanted only peace. Their peace flag, they called it.

Soon, as American tanks rolled through the streets of Altmannstein, blaring loudspeakers repeated over and over the message that their town had surrendered and the war was over. The townspeople were jubilant and welcomed the war-weary G.I.s with warm hospitality. The menacing presence of the SS officers from only days before had vanished, and no one knew nor cared where they had fled.

The American troops' occupation of the little village of Altmannstein was a peaceful one. The only restriction imposed on the townspeople by the occupying commander was a strict curfew. All citizens were to be in their homes by nine p.m. every night while troops patrolled the streets peacefully. After a perfunctory searching of all homes to flush out any renegade Nazis, the Americans settled in and occupied several homes, including the Wenzels' residence.

Maria Wenzel, always the cautious one, decided that it would be prudent for her budding seventeen-year-old daughter to sleep in the attic smokehouse — door firmly locked — while the soldiers were billeted with them. Fortunately, their Jewish friends that had hidden in the smokehouse were now able to start their lives over again without any threat to their safety from the occupying American soldiers.

One of the two officers who quartered in their home, Lieutenant Kauffman, spoke fluent German and so became their translator. That evening the officers returned with a bottle of whiskey and a portable radio. Suddenly the house was filled with singing and laughter once more. The long war had stilled any music for the German citizens, for as long as men were fighting and dying on the front lines, dancing had been strictly forbidden. The only song they had heard all throughout the war was "Lily Marlene," which the state-controlled radio broadcast network played after each newscast.

Now, as they all sat around the dining table sharing their meal with these two smiling Americans, there was a kind of holiday atmosphere, a kindred of spirit.

"To peace!" Lieutenant Kauffman raised his glass in toast, "let this be a celebration of peace."

"To peace," they all echoed.

The little portable radio played softly in the background. The music that the Armed Forces Network played seemed to fascinate Lisl. The swaying melodies of these strange American love songs of 1945 were so vastly different from the Alpine waltzes and yodeling songs that she was used to. It all seemed so modern and glamorous to her, and she couldn't get enough of them.

The other officer, Lieutenant Bob Kingsley, wanted desperately to tell the German family how breathtakingly beautiful he found their countryside. So with the help of Kauffman's painstaking translation, Kingsley described the pristine beauty of Bavarian Germany through the eyes of the conquering Allies. How surprised, he said, the soldiers were to see the gently rolling hills carpeted with native spring flowers: poppies, daisies, bluebells, buttercups, all swaying in the gentle breeze.

And the forests! he said, his blue eyes twinkling. They all seemed so clean, he told them. Not a stick or broken branch in sight. Lisl and her parents smiled to themselves. Little did this young man know that the previous winter had been extremely harsh and, with coal so meagerly rationed, many townspeople scurried into the woods to collect whatever firewood they could find to keep themselves warm. Thus, the clean forests!

After a while, everyone became exhausted from the talking and the laughter, and so, they retired for the night. It seemed to Lisl that the convivial evening had a somewhat elixir effect for their war-torn and weary souls. A kinship of sorts had been formed between the cooperative townspeople and the occupying American officers, and so, the healing process began.

CHAPTER 8

With the American occupation of Germany now fully implemented, the aftermath of the bombing was brought home once again as they listened to the radio describe the devastation that had taken place in major cities like Berlin, Bremen, Nürnberg, and Munich — especially Munich. Frightening reports of civilians trapped alive under the rubble of demolished buildings were everywhere. Munich was virtually paralyzed. It had been weeks since the Wenzels had heard from Maria and her family. Until recently she had always written or called faithfully after each bombing to let them know that she was safe. It seemed no matter how vicious the bombing got, Maria's neighborhood had always miraculously been spared. Now with power lines down, railway tracks destroyed, no communications whatsoever available, they had no way of reaching her or knowing if Maria and her family were even still alive.

It appeared quite a few families had loved ones in Munich, and so, it was decided that a small band of young people, including Lisl, would ride bicycles to Munich, one hundred and six kilometers away, in search of their families. They set out the very next morning at four o'clock — the little ragtag team of cyclers — knapsacks stocked with sandwiches and bottles of lemonade.

There were six of them altogether, four boys and two girls. Lydia, the only other girl in their group, was dark-haired, petite, slight of build, but with powerful legs — well conditioned from farm chores. Hans, Karl, Max and Dieter were tall, strapping schoolmates of Lisl's that, because of their age, had narrowly missed the draft. Each boy, however, had a strong sense of responsibility and family loyalty. They became the men in their families when fathers and older brothers made their sacrifices on the battlefields. Lydia and Lisl let the boys ride in front with Hans in the lead. The vee-shaped formation the boys made served as a wind foil for the two girls.

They knew, at the outset, what a long and arduous journey lay ahead. The muddy roads were deeply rutted, and cavernous holes gaped everywhere as a dramatic testament to the power of the Allies' bombs. Oxen-drawn carts, filled with hay or squawking chickens, with farmers and their kerchiefed wives walking alongside, would pass occasionally as the cyclers stopped to rest by the side of the road.

Oftentimes as they pedaled along in rhythm together, they would all seem lost in their own thoughts. "I hope we find our loved ones alive," Lisl mused more to herself than to anyone in particular.

"It's the only thing that keeps me going," Lydia replied.

"I remember when I was little," Lisl said, "I used to visit my sister Maria in Munich. What a beautiful city it was! She was always so good to me and never failed to show me a good time. If anything has happened to her — I — I don't know what I'll do…" Lisl tried to hold back her tears.

"I know — I know," Lydia answered. "My sister Katherine was — rather, *is* — the same way. We mustn't believe the worst. Let's be optimistic and assume they're all okay. Oh, Lisl, I'm so exhausted."

Hans, who had heard the girls' conversation, yelled over his shoulder to the rest of them, "Let's stop here. We each have one last sandwich left and we've almost reached the city." Grateful for another rest, they all pulled over to the side of the road and settled down in the grass to munch on their snack.

Karl stood up and surveyed their surroundings. "Judging from the landmarks, we're just on the outskirts of Munich," he said. The youngest of three children, Karl had lost both his father and older brother to the war and was now hoping to find his older sister in Munich.

Suddenly a movement from the corner of her eye caught Lisl's attention. Putting down her sandwich, she crawled over to a heap of blue and white striped canvas huddled in the ditch next to them.

"Oh, my God," she cried. "There's a man down here! Hans, come quick. Help me!"

Hans rushed to her side and together they lifted the skeletal man to a sitting position. Lydia grabbed her lemonade and brought it to them, but the stranger's parched lips could not even move enough to drink.

"Here, let me try," Lisl said, pouring a little of the drink into the cupped palm of her hand. She held it up to his mouth, and he was able to wet his lips and take a little of the fluid in his mouth. The striped, pajama-like uniform hung shapelessly on the man's bony frame. His head appeared to have been shaven, but to the young people the most arresting feature of all was the image of his haunted eyes. Sunken deep in their sockets, the stranger's eyes seemed incredibly large with almost a surrealistic quality.

"Where do you suppose he came from?" asked Dieter.

"All I can think of is there's a prison not far from here in Dachau. He was probably a prisoner who escaped from there," said Karl.

Suddenly Lisl remembered the cryptic words of the state inspector that had come to her house to see if she were well enough to work. What monstrous horrors would she have had to endure as this poor man had? she shuddered at the thought.

"I'm sure he doesn't even know that the war is over," mused Lydia.

"We need to get him some help," Lisl said.

"How?" Karl asked, "We can't carry him on our bikes…"

The vacuous eyes of the stranger looked up at them, and Lisl's heart wrenched at his pathetic expression. She knew they had to do something to help him. Standing up to look around she spotted a farmhouse down the road.

"I know — let's carry him over to that house and see if the people that live there can help us — maybe take him to a hospital."

Lisl ran to retrieve her blanket from her bike and quickly unfolded it to fashion a sling for the man to lie in. The man's body was deceivingly light as Lisl and Hans gently lifted him out of the ditch.

"Careful now," she said, fearing that his fragile bones would break if they moved too quickly.

Once at the farmhouse, the youngsters were relieved to find a woman and her grown daughter living there. While the daughter called the Red Cross, the older woman told them that her daughter worked in the nearby hospital and knew not only the doctors at the hospital, but the Red Cross crew as well. Both women assured them that the prison survivor would receive expert medical help.

Before leaving Lisl walked over to the man now lying on the couch and took his hands in hers.

"You'll be safe now, everything's going to be all right," she reassured him gently.

His eyes slowly opened and closed again as if in acknowledgment of her words, and she sensed a slight squeeze of her hand.

Lisl desperately wanted to help, to do more, but she knew she couldn't. It would be the expert medical attention he was to receive at the hospital that would save him. He was badly malnourished — that much was obvious. But his immediate need was for fluids. His severe dehydration had him on the brink of death. Lisl knew, too, that if she and her friends hadn't happened along, he would have most surely perished.

Suddenly an idea struck her. On impulse, she took the necklace from around her neck. Gathering the fine gold chain together, she pressed the small crucifix pendant into his hand.

"My name is Lisl," she said. "Keep this as a little memento from me."

The man looked up at her and weakly squeezed her hand again. She knew then that he would be all right.

The strange paradox of that gesture never occurred to her until many years later — that a young Catholic girl, out of love and compassion for her fellow man, should offer her crucifix to a Jewish concentration camp survivor as a symbol of everlasting faith. Yet, somehow, on that day, it seemed, not only right, but perfectly normal.

One could only speculate as to how he came to that ditch by the side of the road — that he had escaped somehow from nearby Dachau seemed certain. Had he escaped before the liberation by the Allies, or was he one of hundreds of concentration camp survivors who, once the gates were opened by the American troops, ran out into the fields to make his own way back home? The only concern, at the time, for Lisl and her friends, was for his immediate safety and well being.

Wiping the tears away with the back of her hand, Lisl hurried back outside to her waiting comrades. By then the Red Cross had pulled up, and the stranger was whisked away to the hospital.

Slightly shaken and subdued, the six friends mounted their bicycles and continued on their journey once more.

"I hope he'll be all right," Lydia murmured after a brief silence.

"I'm sure he will," Lisl replied. "I'd like to go back later and look him up in the hospital if at all possible to see for myself."

"Perhaps we can. If all goes well and we find our families, we can stop in to see him on the way back," offered Hans.

Suddenly, as they crested a slight rise in the road, the four boys stopped short, and they all stared at the rubble that stretched out before them.

"We're here," said Karl grimly.

"No, it can't be!" cried Lydia. "Where are the buildings, the — the houses?"

Everywhere around them lay the burned-out ruins of tall buildings, churches, stores, museums, now nothing more than useless piles of stone and concrete — grotesque monuments created by some diabolical artist. Here and there were streetcars that had crashed together like giant sheaves of wheat stacked in the midst of the rubble.

"I don't know where we are any longer," Hans said, shaking his head in dismay. "All the landmarks are gone."

"How will we find anybody?" asked Max, the youngest boy in the group.

"Look over there! I believe that's Bahnhofstrasse — and, if it is, I can get us to my sister's house," Lydia offered.

Deciding that her plan would be the best route they could take under the circumstances, they followed Lydia and made their way through the ruins to her sister's apartment. Craters pock-marked the streets. Everywhere they looked there were endless piles of rubble, twisted cables, broken sewer pipes and half-razed apartment buildings with gaping rooms, their furniture hanging precariously in the open air. Part of her apartment building had been destroyed, but, miraculously, the group found Lydia's sister Katherine safe. After a brief, cursory round of introductions, they gratefully accepted her offer to put them up for the night. Her quarters were already cramped with evacuated neighbors, but no one seemed to mind the crowded accommodations. As it turned out, Katherine knew the city quite well, and so, graciously offered to accompany Lisl to Maria's house in the morning or, at the very least, point her in the right direction. The little group made plans that at daybreak they would each go their separate ways and meet back at Katherine's shelter in a week for the return trip home.

Not wanting to waste another minute, Lisl and Katherine set out on their bicycles for Maria's apartment the following morning at daybreak. Lisl had given Katherine the address, and they pedaled determinedly in the direction of Maria's apartment house. All around them, the sweeping devastation of war was almost unbearable.

The two girls hadn't pedaled very far when suddenly Katherine stopped, got off her bike and motioned for Lisl to stop. A funeral procession was crossing their path. Silently they watched as the priest solemnly led the mourners, all clad in black. A trio of altar boys walked slowly behind the priest. The lead altar boy carried high a crucifix that swayed slightly in the breeze. Lisl caught a smoky whiff of incense as the little procession turned into the gates of a nearby cemetery.

"Oh, God, I hope it's not Maria," Lisl whispered anxiously.

Once the last member of the group had walked slowly past them and made it to the grave site, the girls watched quietly as the mourners began to gather around the freshly dug grave. Lisl pressed her face against the ornate wrought iron fence that surrounded the cemetery, craning her neck and fearing that she might recognize a loved one. Anxiously, she searched for a familiar face and all the while praying that she wouldn't find one. Soon, however, her fears were dispelled, and they mounted their bicycles once more.

Before too long the surroundings began to look familiar, and her heart was filled with anticipation. Suddenly there before her, totally untouched, loomed Maria's apartment building, just a block away.

"Well, I think you'll be all right now, won't you," smiled Katherine.

"Thanks for all your help, Katherine."

They shook hands and parted with a casual "*Servus.*" Her knees weak with relief, Lisl pushed herself to pedal even harder that last block until she reached the building. All up and down the wide boulevard the elegant apartment buildings seemed to have been spared from the massive destruction falling from the skies. The stately oak trees lining the avenue were untouched. The tall wrought-iron gate creaked as Lisl opened it. She glanced up to see the ever present flower boxes still spewing forth their riotous colors. Walking across the courtyard past the neatly-trimmed bushes that were growing in stone planters, Lisl trembled as she rang the doorbell. The door opened immediately and, before Lisl knew it, Maria was standing before her. Her eyes flew open wide at the sight of her youngest sister.

"Lisl! Did you ride your bicycle all the way from home?" Maria asked incredulously.

Lisl could only nod, her chin trembling as tears of joy and relief spilled down her cheeks.

"Oh, Maria!" The two sisters hugged and swayed together for what seemed forever. "We thought you'd been killed — there was a funeral," Lisl sobbed, "I was so afraid it was for you — you can't imagine how scared I was." The words spilled forth in an avalanche of emotion.

Later, over tea, Maria explained that she had continued to write home. Unfortunately, her letters never arrived. Her husband, Franz, joined them at the kitchen table, and the three of them chattered away into the night. "We have very little gas or electricity, and we burn newspapers to keep warm, but we manage; we get along," Maria remarked brightly.

Lisl settled back, listening to her sister, and allowed the warmth and love to wash over her as she silently thanked God for keeping her entire family alive and safe throughout the war.

Exactly one week later, as scheduled, Lisl met up with her bicycle friends — all of whom had also successfully found their relatives alive and well. The convivial, upbeat mood of the return trip to Altmannstein was indeed a far cry from the anxiety-ridden journey of a week ago.

As they pedaled along in unison, Hans began whistling the song "The Happy Wanderer." Soon he was joined by Max, who in his pure, strong soprano accompanied him on the chorus. Before too long, the rest of the group joined in — singing in harmony and all the while pedaling in rhythm. Their voices swelled with the lilting strains of the familiar folk song. It was a beautiful, sunny day and their spirits soared as they made their way back home.

As they rounded the bend and Altmannstein came into view, they were delighted to find that the townspeople had turned out en masse to welcome them home. Their good news spread rapidly amongst the families and gladdened the hearts of everyone. The following Sunday at Mass, Father Tempel acknowledged their successful mission and thanked them on behalf of the entire town.

A few weeks later, while Lisl tended to her chores, her mother brought her a letter from Maria, and together they sat down to read it. Her sister Maria assured the family that all was well with her in spite of the hardships. Simple things like coffee, butter, and fresh fruit were still impossible to get. She wrote they had all been drinking ersatz coffee for so long, they've forgotten what the real thing tastes like. Occassionally she would help some of the thousands of war refugees that packed the streets of Munich every day. The soldiers from the 45th Infantry Division that occupied the city of Munich patrolled regularly and maintained a sense of order. The urban populace, she observed, was gradually coming out, dusting itself off, and sweeping away its rubble. Slowly the city, like a giant awakening animal, was beginning to rebuild itself.

Lastly, Maria wrote of her trip to the hospital to check on the prison camp survivor knowing how concerned Lisl had been. She said his name was David Levine and, although he was still in intensive care, the head nurse assured Maria he was expected to make a complete recovery. Lisl wondered, of course, if his psyche would ever make a complete recovery having witnessed and been subjected to the unspeakable horrors of concentration camp life. David explained to Maria during her bedside visit that he had lost his entire family at Dachau, but hoped that one aunt who lived in Munich would still be alive. David also expressed his deepest gratitude to the six young people that found him — especially Lisl, and that he would always keep the necklace as a reminder of the Good Samaritans that saved him.

As a parting request, he gave Maria his aunt's name and address and asked her if she could locate her for him. Unfortunately, when Maria appeared at the address she had been given, she was told that David's aunt had disappeared a year ago, and no one knew where she had gone.

As the days went by, the Wenzel family never failed to include David in their evening prayers. One evening Michael suggested they make another trip into Munich, this time just father and daughter, once again on the motorcycle.

"We'll stop at the hospital to look up your friend David," Michael said.

After a long, satisfying visit with Maria and her husband, Lisl and her father stopped at the hospital just outside Munich. Walking up the stairs of the old hospital building, Lisl wondered how David would look, remembering the sunken eyes and the painfully skeletal body that they had found in the ditch that fateful day. The head nurse led them to the men's ward and pointed to the third row of beds on the right. A frail young man sitting in a chair next to a bed turned and smiled at them.

"Oh, God, You've answered our prayers!" Lisl cried out as she walked over to hug him. He stood up to greet her, and they smilingly gazed at each other. Remembering her manners, Lisl quickly introduced him to her father. The two men shook hands.

Although David was far from the picture of good health, his face had fleshed out remarkably in the short time he had been recuperating. His brown eyes, no longer sunken and cloudy, were large and expressive. His once-shaven head had changed into a closely cropped head of shiny brown hair that gave him a charming schoolboy look. For a fleeting moment, Lisl suddenly found herself wondering what it would be like to dance with him, kiss him under the stars. Shaking her head at her foolish, teenage thoughts, Lisl took his hand and said, "The Lord answered our prayers — thank God you've survived."

"It's because of this," he said, holding up the gold cross necklace she had given him. "I'll never be without it because it will always remind me of the Good Samaritans that rescued me. Now, let's go into the solarium to visit. It's much more pleasant in there," David suggested.

The three of them walked down the tiled hall of the hospital to the glass French doors that opened up into a spacious lounge. Skylights flooded the room with sunshine and luxurious hanging ferns gave it a homey atmosphere. White wicker furniture with bright floral cushions completed the garden look.

"Since the doctors told me my recuperation time would be fairly lengthy, I've started to spend a lot of time here in this room." David said. "It seems to heal my soul as much as my body."

"I can certainly see why," Michael smiled.

Pulling up a chair, Michael continued, "David, I can't tell you how sorry we all are about your family. I know you have nowhere to go when you leave here, is that right?"

"Yes," David sighed, "I suppose I could continue with my studies at the university, although that seems so long ago — before the round up of my family and all…" his voice trailed off.

Lisl shot a glance at her father, hoping he could say something that would bring some comfort to this tortured young man.

"David," Lisl said softly, putting her hand on his knee, "we want to help you."

"Help me? You've already helped me — you saved my life," he replied patting her hand.

"No, we'd like to do more," added Michael offering him the small package he'd been carrying. "This is just some clean clothes and a little money for when you get out of the hospital." Michael had tucked two hundred Deutschmarks in the pocket of the pants he was giving David.

"Once you're out of here, and you decide you want a job, please come to Altmannstein. I'm planning to build a house for my daughter Frieda within the next few months and I could use some help. I'd be proud to have you on my crew. The pay is modest but fair, and I will help you find close accommodations."

Just then a nurse stuck her head in the door. "David, it's time for your medicine," she said with a smile.

"He*rr* Wenzel, you've given me a lot to think about," David said, standing up and offering Michael his hand. "I'll let you know once I'm released from the hospital."

CHAPTER 9

Slowly the everyday life of a country at war evolved into the everyday life of a country at peace. Factories that had quickly converted to munitions plants at the outset of the war were slowly attempting to convert back to crank out appliances, clothing, household goods and everything else associated with the ordinary business of life.

Although the American officers had moved out of the Wenzels' home and into a vacant house shortly after their arrival, it appeared the occupying troops would be staying in Altmannstein for an indefinite amount of time. Thus, some type of recreational activities would have to be found to provide the necessary entertainment and relaxation the soldiers needed. The commanding officer met with the town's *Bürgermeister*r, and it was decided that the old kindergarten in the heart of town could be converted into a serviceable night club. After the occupation was over, the club would eventually be converted back to a kindergarten.

Lieutenant Kauffmann, who had been charged with spearheading the operation asked Maria and Lisl to help decorate the new club by sewing tablecloths and curtains from the yards and yards of white bed sheeting that the Army had available. The two women threw themselves into the project with all the anticipation of a Saturday night dance.

"Are you two enjoying yourselves?" Frieda asked one day as she breezed into the living room where Lisl and her mother were busy sewing.

"Actually, yes. Isn't this exciting?" Lisl answered. "Just think of it, Frieda, a real night club right here in Altmannstein! The lieutenant said there'd be singers and bands brought in, and I might even be able to make a little money waitressing if I wanted to."

"Well, don't get too carried away, Lisl. I heard Gretl down the street telling Berta Stegermeier, that Max, Karl and Hans were not too happy about this. There are rumors that these boys want to grab you and cut off your hair all the way to the scalp for your involvement in all this." Frieda helped herself to some cold cuts on the table and started making a sandwich.

"My *involvement* in all this? What on earth does *that* mean?" Lisl cried.

"Frieda," Maria admonished, "you know as well as we do the war is over now, and we thank God every day that we're all still alive!"

Lisl saw the instant sadness come over Frieda's face as she knew what her sister was thinking. Yes, they were all still alive, but no one knew about her husband Alfons who was still missing. Maria reached out and patted Frieda's hand, "I meant at least *we're* still here. Alfons will come home soon, Honey. At any rate," she continued, "these American soldiers have been pretty decent to us — and we need to maintain our friendship with them and cooperate!"

"*I* know that, Mama, but these boys are so resentful that American men are showing Lisl so much attention, and girls like Gretl are just jealous, that's all," Frieda said with a shrug as she started to bite into her sandwich. "Oh, and Lisl? You should have heard how Berta defended you to that Gretl! She said you were only doing the decent thing, and that by cooperating with the Americans, we can all promote peace and harmony. She even said that she admired you for it and that we could all learn from your actions. Can you imagine?"

"Berta had always been a true friend," Lisl acknowledged, but she was thinking now of what Frieda had said. Could these boys actually physically overcome her and shave off her hair? Having one's hair clipped short was the popular treatment accorded to female traitors. Lisl had read in the papers of some of the Nazi collaborators in France after the American liberation of that country and how the women had been shorn of their locks. She recalled their pictures, the ridiculously short hair, so mannish and ugly, the humiliated, downcast eyes… yes, they were definitely traitors to their country. But not she! The war was over! She was only helping the Americans in the spirit of cooperation because they had asked her to. Surely she could speak to Max and the others about this. Maybe there was some mistake…

The next day, as Lisl stood on a chair to hang the freshly ironed curtains in the window, she spotted Max, Karl and Hans gathering together outside to watch. They whispered and sneered to each other as she pinned and ruffled the material together.

"Don't you guys have something better to do than to stand there and watch? You could come in and help, you know," she yelled amicably out the window to them.

"*We* still have our pride!" Karl retorted. "*We* don't want to do any more than we have to to help our former enemy take over our town."

Lisl laid down the remaining material she held gathered in her arms and strode outside to face them. All three boys stood their ground, their fists clenched, their jaws jutting forward defiantly.

Max looked at her, his gaze never wavering. "You'd better think twice before you help these people out any more, Lisl. You're fraternizing with the enemy, you know," his voice thick with disgust.

"Yeah," Karl chimed in, "You keep this up and you may get your hair chopped off — then who will have you, Miss Smarty? You'll be so ugly no man will want you — not even the Americans! Hah-hah-hah." The three chortled with malicious laughter.

Lisl suddenly thought of everything that she had been through, both in Regensburg and at the munitions factory during the war, and now to be faced with the threat of being sheared like a sheep by these immature, cocky young men was utterly laughable.

"Max," she said, "be reasonable. We all went to school together! How can you threaten me like that? Why, I even had an unbearable crush on you when we were growing up." She relished the dumbfounded look on Max's face as she continued, "Yes, believe it or not, I did. You never knew because you were too busy chasing all the other girls in school. I also admired your intelligence — or, at least, what I thought was intelligence. Now I'm not so sure. Besides, in case you haven't noticed, my friend, the war is over. There is no more *enemy*. Our country has lost its battle, and now we need to make an effort to get along with these Americans."

"Well, you — you just need to stay with your own kind, that's all," he said, pushing a stone around with the toe of this shoe.

"That's for *me* to decide," she replied over her shoulder as she marched back into the club.

"Don't go anywhere alone, Lisl," Hans shouted after her menacingly. "That's all I can tell you."

That evening happened to be the grand-opening night for the club, and Lisl had been invited by Lieutenant Kauffmann as his special guest to join him for dinner.

As she walked through the town in the gathering darkness, she could feel the jeers and taunts of her former classmates at every turn. Suddenly she found herself practically an alien in her own town. Was she so wrong to want to help the Americans with this club? What had gotten into Max and his friends? She knew that at the tender age of seventeen, their budding masculinity was being severely threatened by these good-looking, self-confident American soldiers who had conquered their land and were now living among them.

Lisl looked up from her reverie in time to see the boys standing with a crowd of others at the door of the club, their arms folded defiantly across their chests, their stance displaying their every intent to block her entrance.

"Let me through, please," she said quietly.

The tension was so thick in the warm night air one could almost cut it with a knife. Max reached out to finger a lock of her hair lazily. "You'd look pretty pathetic without your crowning glory, you know."

"Lieutenant!" Lisl called out, her eyes fixed on Max.

"What's going on out here?" Lieutenant Kauffmann asked as he opened the door.

"These guys won't let me by. I wonder if you could give me a hand?" she asked apologetically.

As he moved forward to help her, someone in the crowd shoved the lieutenant, and before anyone knew it, he grabbed one of the ruffians by the shoulder, swung him around and punched him squarely in the jaw.

"You gentlemen need to leave this lady alone," Lieutenant Kauffmann said as the young man picked himself up off the ground, gingerly rubbing his swollen jaw."Now, go home where you belong. I don't want to see any of you hanging around here again!"

The boys scurried away quickly, as the lieutenant escorted Lisl into the club.

"Thank you for saving me like that," she murmured softly, "I'm sorry my friends caused so much trouble. They're really not bad guys; they're just having a tough time adjusting to the occupation, that's all."

"I suspect it will take us all a long time to understand each other," he replied with a smile, "but for now, thank you for your willingness to help us."

The club opened without further incidence, and everyone there seemed to enjoy themselves that night. The main hall of the converted kindergarten had been magically transformed into a modestly elegant night club with a bar at one end and tablecloth'ed round tables scattered around the room. The center of the room became a tiny polished parquet dance floor. Lisl looked around the room and beamed with pride. The five-piece orchestra sat rehearsing a ballad that was popular Stateside.

See the Pyramids along the Nile
Watch the sunrise on a tropic isle,
Just remember, Darling, all the while
You belong to me.

Lisl swayed to the mellow strains and imagined a handsome young officer taking her in hand and leading her to the dance floor.

She shook her head and smiled inwardly at her adolescent fantasies.

The bartender winked at her as he leaned on the bar polishing imaginary smudges from an already spotless tumbler. Lisl felt the scarlet heat quickly rise on her cheeks as she realized she'd been caught day-dreaming. Nevertheless, she thought, the music was good, and the lieutenant had been right, the touring bands that the Army was bringing in would lend an air of sophistication to the atmosphere. Once again, Lisl felt proud that she had been a part of it all.

One early morning in the summer of '45, Michael sent Anne and Lisl out into the vegetable fields that they maintained on the outskirts of town to tend to the potato crop. Maria had had another severe asthma attack, and Michael wanted to stay home to be with her. Anne had been quiet and withdrawn after learning that Ludwig had been captured by the Allies, and all of them prayed each day that they would receive word from him or, at least, learn of his whereabouts now that the war was over. Tragically, no word came, and Anne was rapidly becoming a mere shell of her former self.

It hurt Lisl to see her closest sister wasting away with grief, and she tried constantly to cheer her up and cajole her out of her glumness.

"Hey, you old grouch," Lisl yelled at her, playfully flinging a dirt clod at her as she bent over a potato plant. The clod hit her squarely on the derriere with a soft thud.

"Don't *do* that," Anne said with a tinge of irritation in her voice. "I'm not in the mood to play, okay? Let's just get these potato bugs picked so we can get back to the house."

The two continued to work the fields in silence. The sun climbed higher in the clear blue sky, and the only sound heard was the droning of the bees in the hot, still air.

"Let's take a break and eat our lunch," Lisl suggested, wiping her brow, "we've finished this section and only have ten more rows to go."

They walked down to the brook that ran through the family's vegetable garden and settled down on the grassy bank to eat their sandwiches. The crystal clear water looked inviting as it sparkled and swirled over the sun-dappled stones.

After they finished eating, Anne leaned back, lifted her heavy auburn hair off her neck and said, "I can't believe how hot it is this summer."

"I know, and it's not even August yet," Lisl replied as she languidly trailed long blades of grass in the bubbling water. Off in the hazy distance, an Army convoy made its way along the country road leading into town. The two women both leaned back on their elbows and watched the convoy pass. The countryside looked quiet and peaceful in the noonday sun, and Lisl watched through half-closed eyes as heat shimmers seemed to melt the road leading off into the horizon.

Suddenly Anne sat upright and froze, her hand flying to her throat.

"What is it?" Lisl asked.

The color drained from Anne's face as she stared out at the road. Lisl turned to follow her gaze, her eyes squinting against the sunlight. A lone figure, stoop-shouldered and incredibly thin, was slowly limping along the road. As the stranger came into view, Lisl could see that he was in some kind of pain, although she couldn't make out his face.

"Who is that, do you know?"

"It's Ludwig," Anne said, her voice cracking.

"What?" It couldn't be, Lisl thought, Ludwig was too robust, too hearty to be this frail stranger.

By now Anne had already jumped up and was running towards him, waving her hand to catch his attention.

"Ludwig! Ludwig!" She called out as she stumbled and ran across the field.

He turned in her direction and his face broke out in that unmistakable lopsided grin that had always endeared him to the family. He started limping toward her waving his arms as well.

Tears welled in Lisl's eyes as she watched the couple throw their arms around each other, kissing and hugging and crying.

"I've missed you so," Anne cried, frantically taking his face in her hands and showering him with kisses.

Closing his eyes and holding his wife tight, Ludwig whispered, "I can't believe I made it at last... I made it... I'm home!"

Reluctant to intrude on their reunion, Lisl shyly came up behind her sister and said, "Hello, Ludwig, remember me?"

"Lisl! How you've grown! Look at you!" He held her at arm's length, then gathered her up in a big, friendly bear hug. Lisl felt his sharp shoulder blades and realized his strength belied his frailty. He felt so light, so incredibly light in her arms. The three of them finally collected their things and walked home arm-in-arm.

That evening as they sat around the table at the Wenzel's home, Ludwig told them how he had been captured by the Allies early on in the war and kept in a P.O.W. camp for the duration. Ludwig had been in the infantry, and on that fateful day in '43, his platoon had surrounded a French garrison in the Ardennes Forest near Le Catelet, France. They had bombarded the emplacement with round after round of mortar fire. After all returning clatter of machine gun fire had ceased, Ludwig and four of his comrades were sent to the front of the battle to assess the damages. As he and the other soldiers ran out from the forest, they were met with a surprise attack of heavy gunfire. Ludwig watched helplessly as his comrades fell around him. Quickly he crawled over to where one of his fellow soldiers lay and lifted the man onto his shoulders to carry him to safety. As he headed for a shallow ravine, he felt the burning sear of shrapnel tear through his leg. Unable to walk he and the other wounded soldiers were then quickly rounded up and marched to the Allies' field headquarters from where they were then transferred to a small P.O.W. camp somewhere in France. Although weak and fatigued, he was grateful to his captors for not mistreating or torturing him and his downed comrades. Horror stories were already circulating even in France of how the Russians were treating their German captives. The torture and inhumane treatment of P.O.W.s by the Russians made a complete mockery of the Geneva Convention.

No, he related to them, his only formidable foe from that point on was boredom. To keep his spirits up and make time pass quicker, he said, he often spent evenings playing cards with some of the American soldiers that maintained the camp. They all smiled as they envisioned Ludwig shuffling cards at a makeshift poker table, his uniform cap set at a rakish angle on his head and a cigarette dangling from his lips. Only Ludwig, with his indomitable charm, could befriend his American captors, and ease the pain and loneliness of a P.O.W.camp for his fellow prisoners and captors alike.

Once Germany surrendered and the war was over, the German

P.O.W.s were free to find their own way back home. Ludwig spent days walking and hitchhiking across Germany, sometimes sleeping in the open fields under the stars. Other times he'd find abandoned farmhouses or barns, but his one thought always was to make it home. He had caught shrapnel in his leg during his capture, but the camp doctor told him he would fully recover.

Now with Lisl's family almost complete, the only missing member was Alfons, her sister Frieda's husband. Their first word of him during the war was that he was classified as missing in action, presumably also captured by the Allies.

"Ludwig," Frieda asked anxiously, "did you happen to hear of Alfon's whereabouts while you were in that prison camp?"

"No, I'm sorry, Frieda," Ludwig replied. He got up to sit down next to her on the couch and put his arm around her shoulders. "I tried to find out whatever I could, but they just didn't have any information — I'm sorry," he whispered.

Frieda straightened and managed a smile. During the war Frieda had received a postcard from Dieter Krause, a buddy of Alfons, who had also been captured by the Americans and was kept in a P.O.W.camp in Texas. Dieter told Frieda that the last he had seen of Alfons was when a group of them were being transported to various camps and, in the process, Dieter and Alfons became separated. Dieter wound up in the prison camp in Texas, and he did not know where Alfons ended up.

Shortly after the war was over, Frieda received one more postcard, this time from Alfons himself. In short cryptic words he let her know he was in a prison camp somewhere in Russia, and that was the last she'd heard from him.

As it were, it would be four more years before the family was to see Alfons again. When he did finally come home, he explained that he and Dieter got separated when the Americans decided they had too many German prisoners and so, apparently traded some of the men to the Russians. Alfons suspected at the time what was happening, he said, because the compass he kept taped to his chest indicated that he was headed east, not west. His remaining years of captivity now spent in the Russian camp was a living hell and took every ounce of strength he had to maintain his sanity and survive. Forced to march endless miles in knee-deep snow, he watched helplessly as comrades around him collapsed and died of exposure, their bodies frozen in the snow. Once encamped, the surviving German prisoners were then subjected to countless humiliations and atrocities such as being forced to eat their own excrement smeared on bread, for the sheer entertainment of their Russian captors.

Through it all, Alfons never gave up hope and was determined to survive and make it home at all costs. It took four long years and it was only because of the new chancellor Konrad Adenauer's efforts to settle the issue of the remaining P.O.W.s with the Soviet Union. Finally, in late 1949, Alfons came back home to Altmannstein, and to his family that had awaited this day, his homecoming was all the more jubilant.

CHAPTER 10

World War II, at least in Europe, was finally over. The conquered land was at peace once more. Lisl's family had survived intact, and for that she thanked the Lord every day. Now it was time to get on with her life.

It was August 1945. She was almost eighteen and ready to venture out into the working world alone. The occupying soldiers were a fact of life for them now. Like it or not, the familiar green Army uniforms were everywhere. One grew accustomed to seeing G.I.'s in shops, on the streets, and in restaurants and taverns. Most Germans were faced with the monumental task of rebuilding their shattered lives and so were learning to live with the routine of military convoys rolling through their towns; G.I.s milling about in stores; American tanks performing maneuvers on distant hills, and all the other facets of life in an occupied country. Those of Lisl's countrymen who recognized the stark realities of living under the rule of another nation learned to speak English, learned to be hospitable to the ever-present American soldier and, in short, learned to live again. Those who harbored resentment and mourned the loss of their proud country's freedom, harbored and mourned in silence.

As for Lisl, she was on the brink of adulthood, and the world lay before her in all its excitement and wonder. Many of her girlfriends had already found jobs with some of the military installations now popping up in neighboring cities.

Sitting outside in the bright sunshine, one Sunday afternoon she listened to Trudi Hofer describe her newfound career with an army post in Vilseck-Grafenwöhr. The fragrance of gladioli, snapdragons and carnations hung thickly in the warm sun-drenched air. Lisl's mother, like other residents of Altmannstein, had made the most of each patch of ground available for planting. The few square yards of garden were crammed with long-stemmed flowers of every variety. A narrow but tidy little walkway cut through the flowers and led to a sturdy bench fashioned from smooth, white birch branches that were lashed together.

"Lisl, they train you for any job you might be interested in and, believe me, there's plenty of work. The Americans are looking for people to hire on the post," Trudi said.

Lisl watched as her friend talked non-stop, her eyes shining with excitement. Trudi had left Altmannstein right after graduation. Lisl remembered her fondly as the painfully shy younger sister of Stefan. Now sitting in Maria's flower garden, the sunlight bouncing off her newly waved hair in sparkling glints, she seemed a totally different girl — older, more sophisticated and polished. Lisl wondered how three short months of life in the city could have wrought such a change in a person. Trudi had been one of Lisl's many school chums who, like many young bright Germans, took advantage of the post-war job market that opened up to anyone who wanted to take advantage of it.

"I'm not sure my parents would want me to live so far away," Lisl said.

"It's not that far. . . besides you could room with me, and we could come home together on weekends with my new boyfriend. He has a car, you know," Trudi replied. She eyed Lisl with a curiously smug, little half-smile.

It all sounded exciting and wonderful and terribly grown up to Lisl, but at the same time, it was a bit frightening. Her wartime experiences away from home had all been horrifying and traumatic. Somehow the warmth of her parent's home was still a source of comfort to her.

"I'm not sure what I could do on the post — if I could even find a job..." she murmured hesitantly.

"Oh, Lisl, they need secretaries, clerks, translators, even switchboard operators like me. I could get you in so easily," Trudi went on, the excitement in her voice building. "My apartment is not far from the post — actually within walking distance — and I really could use the help with the rent if you split it with me... Please say you'll come?"

"What about my English?" Lisl asked "I've only picked up a little bit from Lieutenant Kauffman." The occupying American commander had taken her under his wing somewhat in the months following the surrender and taught her the rudiments of basic English.

Trudi tossed her dark hair back and laughed, "You'll do just fine. You'll be surprised how quickly you pick it up once you're surrounded by it every day."

How could she lose? Lisl thought. Trudi's plan made perfect sense to her and, surprisingly enough, her parents were agreeable to allowing her to move in with her friend and begin the search for a job on the post in Vilseck-Grafenwöhr.

And so that fall, Lisl began a new life as an adult, in a strange new world, surrounded by Americans. She marveled at their culture — these smiling, tanned and easy-going Americans. Lisl and Trudi made friends easily with not only the bachelor servicemen they came to know, but also the young WACs and WAFs that were stationed at these new Army and Air Force installations. Bright, good looking young women dedicated to serving their country, but always warm and friendly to their civilian hosts. Weekends would often find the two young Germans sightseeing with a handful of American friends, all of them laughing and chattering at the same time. Lisl and Trudi were the tour guides and sometime-interpreters in shops and restaurants as they explored the cities and countryside with their American military friends.

Finding a job was the easiest part of all: Trudi accompanied Lisl to the employment office on the post, and, after a few obligatory questions, all of which she answered in English, she was suddenly a new overseas switchboard operator ready to report immediately to the Third Army Headquarters Signal Office in Vilseck-Grafenwöhr.

The girls' apartment was a two-bedroom walk-up situated in a quiet neighborhood thick with elm and maple trees. By pooling their meager paychecks, Lisl and Trudi managed to pay the bills and put food on the table — most of the time. There were times when the money ran out, but the month had not, and so, the two lived on whatever food they had left in the apartment. It was at times like this that their landlady, a motherly sort named *Frau* Apfel, would bring up a warm tureen of potato soup or an extra loaf of bread she had picked up at the bakery. In spite of the occasional hard times, Lisl was happily enjoying her new life and her new-found independence.

Weekend trips home were always a special pleasure. Michael never failed to fill Trudi's boyfriend's car with sacks of potatoes, huge smoked hams, boxes of home-baked cookies, and other luxuries the girls came to associate with home.

That particular winter of 1945 was one of the coldest on record. To make matters worse, defunct munitions factories were slow in converting back to the textile factories they had been before the war. Warm clothing was scarce. Out of desperation, Lisl traded her beloved accordion on the black market for a fur coat since, by then, the German mark had dropped in value and was considered practically worthless.

She felt sad as she handed over the accordion in return for the coat. So long ago, it seemed Lisl had tried to convince her father that she needed a piano ever since that delightful visit to Munich when she first laid eyes on the fabulous Bechstein in Maria's apartment. But, as hard as Michael tried, there were no pianos available to purchase. All manufacturing had already been focusing on the production of armaments and even small hand crafting industries, like the building of pianos, had dwindled due to lack of demand. The next best thing that Michael could offer his youngest daughter to satisfy her musical yearning was an accordion. Truly Lisl was grateful because, although her father never told her, she was painfully aware of the financial sacrifice her family had to make just to afford the accordion, much less a piano. Now, even *that* musical instrument would be lost to her forever just to keep warm and protected in this harsh and bitter cold.

Lisl and Trudi volunteered to work every shift they could so that they could send money home to their folks as often as possible.

They knew full well that the severe winter was taking its toll on their parents as well. Furthermore, they had, on occasion, borrowed money from their parents to see them through the lean times, and it was important to Trudi and Lisl to pay them back. Therefore, Lisl was only slightly disappointed when she learned she had drawn the graveyard shift Christmas Eve. She had no way to go home for Christmas, anyway, Lisl thought, so she might as well stay on the post, work the late shift, and earn what she could.

Lisl reported to work that night feeling a little melancholy. Christmas carols were being broadcast on the loudspeakers outside as she hurried toward the building. The cheery Christmas lights adorning the drab gray offices of the Communications Building only enhanced her feelings of loneliness as she hung up her new coat and took her seat at the switchboard. Putting on her headset, she soon fell into the rhythm of connecting and disconnecting calls as needed while practicing her English in the smooth, flawless style she had worked hard to perfect.

After a while the switchboard fell silent and her job became a waiting game — waiting for the next call, whenever that might be. The minutes turned into hours as the long, quiet night stretched ahead. Christmas Eve, and she was alone. Everyone at home would be celebrating right about now. Her mother would surely have her *Glühwein* steaming and ready to enjoy. Lisl could almost smell the warm gingerbread cookies her mother always baked. She laid her head back against her chair and closed her eyes for only a moment — her subconscious drifting somewhere between wakefulness and sleep. Laughing faces from her youth floated before her: old girlfriends from school, Stefan Hofer, her three sisters, her parents, all reflecting a happier time before the war.

Suddenly a noise from the hall startled her from her reverie. Lisl sat upright in her chair and strained to listen. Was it real or had she just imagined it? The rustling noise started again, this time closer. Just then the door slowly opened and a three-foot spruce Christmas tree was pointed straight towards her. Lisl stared at the tree in disbelief, and then she saw the tall figure holding it. In the dim light she could see the shine of the insignia on his lapels and realized it was the Officer On Duty making his rounds.

"Merry Christmas," he said with a smile.

"You almost scared me to death," Lisl laughed.

"How are things going tonight?" he asked as he placed the tree on a small table by the window.

"It's going well. Just kind of quiet around here at this time of night."

"Mind if I sit down? You look like you could use some company." The handsome officer pulled up a chair and then offered his hand, "I'm Lieutenant Al Daughtery."

"Lisl Wenzel," she said shaking his hand.

"I'll be right back," he said. Suddenly he jumped up from his chair and disappeared only to return with a large box of doughnuts.

"Thought you might like something to eat," he offered as he went about the task of making coffee in the small percolator standing on the table.

As they silently sipped their coffee and munched on the doughnuts, Lisl regarded him surreptitiously. She watched the officer as he made himself comfortable and realized right away that this man was someone special. Tall, with blue black hair and impossibly handsome, he carried himself with the easy grace of someone accustomed to getting his way in life. His brown eyes seemed to dance with amusement as he watched her bite into a freshly baked doughnut.

Yearning for a friendly face on such a lonely night, she welcomed his companionship. Al was easy to talk with. She felt oddly comfortable with him now and totally captivated by his stories. He told her of his boyhood, of growing up on a reservation in Oklahoma, the youngest of three children. His parents had been full-blooded Cherokee. Both had died, he said, when Al was only eight. It was hard to remember his father. Al felt certain that he had been a proud man. But, slowly, a little at a time, the state and the federal government had taken everything away from his people — his ancestors. All that was left was defeat and the shame that came with it — shame for having nothing, shame for living on a small patch of reserved land. Once the eagle had flown free — proud and free — over mountains and canyons. Land that belonged to the Cherokee was now no more. His father, like his grandfather before him, found his hopelessness in the bottom of a whiskey bottle and had drowned in it. His mother, he felt sure, had died from a broken heart.

Lisl listened earnestly while Al spoke. Looking straight ahead, he spoke quietly, slowly in an even drone. From Oklahoma, he and his older brother and sister moved to Utah to live with a kind, old aunt. Lisl looked into his eyes, now distant and far away, and tried to picture the frightened little eight-year-old boy trying so hard to be brave and her heart ached with tenderness.

"Were you happy in U-," she hesitated, "Utah?"

"Happy enough, I suppose. Children are so resilient, you know. They bounce back from all kinds of adversity. I did vow, from then on, that I would make something more of myself. That I would not let what happened to my father happen to me." Why was he telling her all this? he thought. She was a total stranger. Yet, something about her, the openness of her face, the wonder in her eyes. Oh, those eyes! — the color of the sea — and just like the sea, a man could drown in those eyes. He would have to approach her cautiously. She was like a wide-eyed, long-legged doe, and he didn't want to frighten her off by coming on too strong. His usual lines just would not do with this one. He caught a subtle whiff of her perfume, Chanel Number Five. Yes, Al thought, this girl's special.

"Please continue," she said softly when he had paused to look at her.

"I learned at an early age that I wasn't going to let life defeat me the way it had defeated my ancestors." His mouth hardened into any angry line. "Indian or no Indian, I was going to be somebody. So, I studied hard, made good grades. Good enough, at least, to get me into OCS. And here I am, on the other side of the ocean," he smiled at her, "talking to a gorgeous blonde at four in the morning."

Lisl lowered her eyes and felt the warm crimson blush creep up her cheeks.

"Tell me a little about yourself now," Al said, leaning back in his chair, his hands clasped behind his head.

"Well, my past isn't nearly as exotic or as dramatic as yours sounds," she began. She proceeded to tell him a few things about herself, her loving parents, her interests, her desire to learn impeccable English. Wisely, she kept her war experiences to herself, at least for now. Through it all he seemed enchanted, watching her mouth as she talked. Although a stranger, she felt she could tell him her most intimate secrets, and somehow, he would understand. She knew instinctively that he would never laugh at her no matter what she said. They talked until the sun peeked in the window and her shift was up.

Finally, Al stood up and stretched himself to his full six-feet-five-inches height and said, "I need to get going. You've held me captive with your charm long enough, you fair-haired vixen."

"Really, Lieutenant? I thought it was the other way around," Lisl shot back with a smile.

He leaned close to her and said, "Did you know that when you smile your whole face seems to light up."

Lisl rolled her eyes at the obvious line but was secretly pleased that Al enjoyed their visit together as much as she had.

Coming home that morning she hummed a tune softly under her breath. "You sure are in a good mood for someone who's been working all night," Trudi remarked, arching an eyebrow. She was getting ready to go to work and was standing in the living room ironing a blouse when Lisl came in.

"Oh, the Officer On Duty came by and kept me company for most of the night," she answered trying to keep a nonchalant look on her face.

Trudi chuckled as the iron hissed and sputtered. "You've got that dreamy I'm-in-love look on your face."

"I didn't know it showed."

"Well, it does. So tell me about this wonderful O. D. you met."

Lisl proceeded to tell Trudi what she knew about the charming Lieutenant Daughtery which, she realized, wasn't nearly enough. After all, she had just met him.

"I don't know, Trudi, there was something about him. I know I just met him, and I don't really know that much about him. But, Heaven help me, he affected me like no other man I've ever known."

Was it really possible? Was it possible to be swept away by a man? To fall helplessly, wildly into this euphoric state all because another person had opened his soul to you and in doing so, touched yours so deeply?

"Lisl, be realistic. You've never *really* known any man. What have you to compare him to?"

Lisl started to open her mouth when Trudi quickly explained. "Oh, I know you cared deeply for Stefan, but, honestly, Lisl, that was really just puppy love. Think about it, you were only fifteen. What did you know about love? Oh, sure, you were swept away by my brother in his uniform... He did look terribly dashing in the pictures he sent us, didn't he?" Her eyes misted and a faraway gaze crossed her face for a moment, "but, I just always felt that the two of you were too young, too innocent to make any commitment to each other." Trudi acknowledged the disbelieving look on Lisl's face, "Yes, even Stefan at the ripe old age of eighteen, I thought, was too young. You both would have needed to get to know other people had Stefan lived and had your love been given a chance to bloom. I'm just saying, you need to go slow with this prince-in-shining-armor of yours."

Lisl's roommate Trudi, the pragmatic, had been a classic friend in every sense of the word. Now she was trying to keep her friend's feet planted firmly on the ground when all Lisl wanted to do was sing to the skies, and watch her soul soar with the exhilaration of a once-in-a-lifetime love. Trudi's words made her think of Stefan. How long ago that seemed! Almost as if it were on another planet, in another era. Yet it had only been two years ago! What would Stefan think if he had known that Lisl was falling in love with one of their country's former enemy? She smiled to herself. Stefan will always occupy a little corner of her heart. He was part of her youth, part of the process of growing up, learning to love...and learning to live with tragedy. So much had happened since those innocent days when she and Stefan strolled the romantic walks of Altmannstein... Regensburg... Irene... the bombing, and then that horrid time in the munitions factory. Fortunately, it now seemed a short time and the end was in sight. Lisl didn't think she could have stood a moment longer in that awful place. Nevertheless, she was here now, and an amazing man named Alvin Daughtery had entered her life, and nothing will ever be the same.

"You know, the Italians have a word for what's happened to you: 'Thunderstruck,'" said Trudi.

"I'm what?" Lisl asked skeptically.

"Thunderstruck," she said matter-of-factly. "It means love at first sight. Not that I believe in it myself, but that's what it's called, anyway."

"You don't believe in love at first sight?"

"Oh, please," she scoffed.

"Well, I know now for a fact that it is possible," Lisl declared as she sat down on the couch. She reached for a dishtowel from the clothes basket and began folding it.

"I believe it's fine for romance magazines and novels and such, but not real life."

"Well, maybe, that's just because it hasn't happened to you yet," Lisl said.

Suddenly, she felt sorry for poor Trudi. She wanted so much for her dearest friend to find a wonderful man like Al. Trudi had been dating a young major from New York. Tony certainly treated her well, and it was obvious that he adored her. But for Trudi, as she put it, there were no bells going off in her head when they kissed. Now Lisl hoped with all her heart that Trudi would find someone that made those bells ring endlessly just as they had for her with Al.

Lisl didn't see the handsome lieutenant again for a week and so never gave it much thought when the phone in the hallway of their apartment building rang, and *Frau* Apfel knocked on their door with a message for her.

"A young man is on the phone for you, Lisl — an American," the landlady said with a knowing smile.

"Could this be the tall, dark and handsome Prince Charming you've been talking about," teased Trudi over her shoulder as she stood at the sink washing dishes.

Lisl tossed her dish towel at Trudi and ran downstairs to take the call. It seemed there was a floor show that Friday night at the American-Civilian Club, and Al wanted to take her to it.

"Oh, yes," Lisl said breathlessly, "I'd love to go. But — wait — I don't have a party dress..." It had been so long since Lisl had even dreamed of going to a party, and her pre-war German dresses were hopelessly out of style for something so sophisticated as a floor show at an American nightclub.

"Honey, you're so beautiful you'd look good in a burlap sack! I'll pick you up at eight," Al laughed.

Fortunately, Trudi came through for her by loaning her a smart, black, fitted skirt, and a sea green blouse with black satin trim.

Friday night finally came. When Al picked her up, his eyes lit up and he gave a soft wolf-whistle in appreciation.

"Holy Toledo!" he said, "that green is your color. Your blouse matches your eyes exactly. You'll be the prettiest belle at the ball."

"What do you mean 'belle at the ball'?" Lisl asked in confusion. "Are we going to a ball?"

Al threw his head back and laughed, "It's just an American expression," he said, "you'll get used to it. Come on — we don't want to be late."

As he escorted her to the car, Lisl realized that she had so much to learn about this strange and sometimes contradictory language.

Once seated at their table at the nightclub, Lisl was wide-eyed with wonder at the sights and sounds all around her. She felt as if she had been transported into a magical kingdom, and she was a fairy tale princess. Al was taking particular pleasure in showing her the delights of American leisure life. His eyes sparkled as he magnanimously ordered for the two of them from the heavy, leather-bound menu.

Soon tuxedoed waiters hovered around them serving their dinner with a flourish. Dishes like shrimp cocktail and southern chicken-fried steak which, at first, were totally foreign and exotic to her, soon became favorites for both Al and Lisl.

The show itself was dazzlingly spectacular with colorful costumes and beautiful show girls in feathered headdresses all set against the backdrop of a full orchestra playing toe-tapping Broadway tunes.

After the floor show was over, the lights dimmed and the orchestra quickly attuned itself to the intimate setting by taking up the familiar love songs of the times. The dance floor quickly filled with couples all dancing cheek to cheek to the muted strains of Harry James's "I'll Get By As Long As I Have You." Lisl watched longingly as couples moved about the floor. The women were so glamorous all clad in silk and satin cocktail dresses. Many of the men were in dress uniforms — flashes of olive green and beige mingled with the black tuxedoes of the waiters.

"What are you thinking about?" Al asked. He had been watching her across the small black table.

"Oh, I'm not sure you want to know," she said, twirling the stem of her glass pensively.

"I'm a pretty good listener," he offered.

Lisl tried to collect her thoughts before she spoke, and then said, "All these people here look so relaxed and happy — as if they've never known a care in the world. My background is so different! It was only a few short months ago that I had to run into a bomb shelter to keep from being killed by all the bombing done by the Allies. And now I'm here watching, perhaps, the same men that piloted those planes dancing with their wives or girlfriends, and everything is supposed to be wonderful again. I — I guess I just don't understand war."

"Lisl," Al began, gently taking her hand, "no one understands war or why we do what we do. All we can hope for is that the powers that be guide us all toward a noble goal of world peace that's everlasting.

"I'm just a soldier," he continued, "doing what my country has asked me to do. You're a German girl who has survived the atrocities inflicted on you by both your country's leaders and mine. We're really just small bit players in this theater of life. But you know what?" he said leaning across the table.

"What?" she replied.

"I'm glad we found each other."

Lisl looked up at him and took in the big frame, the broad shoulders, the strong face.

"I'm glad, too," she said.

Just then the orchestra began to play "It Had to Be You."

"May I have this dance?" Al asked.

Lisl could only nod, her heart beating with excitement. A small white spotlight cleaved the dark room. He held her elbow lightly as he led her to the dance floor — tall and dashing in his uniform, Al turned the head of every woman in the room with his arresting good looks. Lisl knew from the start, one look at him and any other man she might have known before paled in comparison. Expertly, without rushing, he took her in his arms, and together they glided across the floor. They danced close together. Lisl certainly didn't consider herself an expert dancer, but she was able to match her movements to Al's. Soon they were dancing as one, swaying to the soft crescendos of the music. As he gazed deeply into her eyes, the other couples on the floor seemed to melt away as if by magic.

Suddenly there was no one around except Al, Lisl and the music. Their feet barely touched the floor, and they were suspended in time. He smiled as his chin rested against her head, and she felt the warmth of his body so close to hers. The subtle aroma of tobacco and spice lingered pleasantly in the air as she closed her eyes. She wanted the song to go on forever. But, to Lisl's dismay, it was over all too soon, and the pair sat down again.

"Want to go outside for a little fresh air?" Lisl's handsome date asked.

"I'd love to," she murmured.

As they walked out into the crisp night air, Al slipped his arm protectively around her waist, and she instinctively leaned closer to him. Lisl was amazed at how natural and right it felt to be with him, as if they had been destined to be as one. It was as if, perhaps in another life, they had been twins. The couple stood on the terrace overlooking the moonlit garden.

After a while, Al put his hands on her shoulders, turning her toward him and said, "You're the most wonderful girl I've ever known, and I think I've fallen in love with you."

Lisl could only murmur, "Really... I don't know what to say."

"You know I'm crazy about you, Lisl. Tell me you feel the same way about me. Tell me," he whispered.

Lisl's eyes filled with tears of happiness as he wrapped his arms around her. He pulled her close and murmured endearments all the while covering her face with slow, soft kisses.

He hadn't even kissed her mouth yet, and already she felt aching desire course through her body in an unstoppable tidal wave. "I love you, Al," she responded turning her face up and meeting his lips in a long, passionate kiss. She felt a dizzying warmth spread through her body in a not entirely unpleasant way. They pulled apart and looked at each other for a moment.

He then pulled her to him again. "Let me take care of you, Darling," he whispered in her hair, "I'll keep you safe and warm forever."

CHAPTER 11

The lifestyle that Lisl and Trudi had together as young bachelorettes struggling to make a living allowed little time for ruminating on any romantic relationship. They shared a pleasant existence for which their moderate means barely sufficed. When they weren't working, they were sleeping, and yet somehow, they still managed to find time for those wonderful weekend trips home to Altmannstein.

On a bright Saturday in the Spring of 1946 as they rounded the familiar corner of the road that led into Altmannstein, Trudi remarked, "Look at all the new construction going on. It seems as if everyone is trying to rebuild out of the ruins of the war — or make things new and clean again, don't you think?"

Amidst the clatter of hammering and sawing, Lisl smiled and said, "Father is building a house for Frieda next door to ours. I'm so eager to see it."

The new house next door had already been framed and bricked when Lisl and Trudi walked up the hill to the Wenzel house.

"Hi, Lisl," she heard a voice from above her call out.

Looking up her eyes met the friendly gaze of David Levine who was attaching tiles to the roof of the new structure.

"David! What a wonderful surprise to see you!" Lisl exclaimed, shielding her eyes from the sun. "This is my friend Trudi Hofer."

Trudi flashed him her dazzling smile and waved hello. As they started to go into the house, David said, "It's almost break time, so come back outside in a little while and we'll visit."

Soon the young people were chattering together in the front yard like old school chums — joking and bantering with each other in a familiar, friendly manner.

That evening a *volksfest* was scheduled to take place in a park on the outskirts of town. David came over to Lisl after the crew cleaned up from the day's work and said, "Do you and Trudi want to go to the *volksfest* with Joe and me for a little while this evening?" Joe, a stocky, curly-haired boy of eighteen, was the bricklayer of the crew and had immediately befriended David when he joined the construction crew.

"We'd love to," Lisl replied, answering for the both of them.

"After everything that's happened to me, it'll be so strange to go somewhere where there's nothing but music and fun again. I — I'm not sure that I'll be the life of the party, but I'd like to at least go and try to forget my problems a little," David mused.

Lisl watched him as he gathered his tools together from the yard and placed them neatly in a wheelbarrow. "David, do you want to talk about your experiences to me sometime? I'll be glad to listen if you ever want to tell me about it."

David looked at Lisl for a long time, and an overwhelming sadness came over his eyes. "No, the International Red Cross has tried to help as many of us camp survivors as they can with clothing, medical help, food — they've even put us in touch with several Jewish agencies, but, you know, no one has come up with any emotional or mental aid that could help us deal with the horrors we experienced. I think, my best bet is just to try to forget. Maybe tonight's *Volkfest* will help me do that. I must say, your father has been a tremendous help to me. Besides giving me a real job and paying me well for it, he's helped me find a room at a boarding-house close by. The landlady there has made it her mission to fatten me up with her good cooking."

Lisl smiled. "Well, if you ever need someone to talk to, I'm here."

Later that evening, as the four of them walked down the moonlit cobblestone road towards the park, they could hear the faint music, laughter and singing coming from the *volksfest*. Once there, they were swept up in the magic of a Bavarian festival: hundreds of people crowded under a huge striped tent; a small stage had been set up in the back where the "oompah" band was thumping out a lively folk song. Lights were strung up all around the periphery of the area, and food vendors were busy trying to keep up with the crowds of people ordering smoked sausage, crisp, warm pretzels, and huge platefuls of cold cut sandwiches. Dirndl'd waitresses were hefting beer steins — four to five in each hand — over the heads of their customers. The two couples found places to sit at one of the long tables and soon were linked arm-in-arm swaying from side-to-side as they sang along.

As the evening drew to a close, Joe turned and said to David, "You and Lisl go on. Trudi and I are going to stay a little longer. Then we'll be along later." It was obvious that Joe was smitten with the vivacious Trudi, having been awed by her elegant American clothes and her sophisticated manner. Lisl and David walked hand-in-hand down the quiet street that led back into town and on to her parents' house. It was late and the streets were quiet. All the windows of the houses they passed were shuttered tight against the night air. Off in the distance somewhere a dog barked.

"Lisl, you'll be interested to know I've decided to go back to school next year," David said after a while.

"Oh, David, how wonderful for you — it's what you've been wanting to do for a long time, isn't it?"

"Yes... but, I was hoping...that is... well, what I'm trying to say is I was hoping that somehow you would be part of my life."

They stopped walking, but David continued to hold Lisl's hand in his. They gazed into each other's eyes only briefly before his head bent down to find her mouth. The kiss was achingly warm and sweet, but to Lisl it lacked the fire of her first embrace with Al. She held David in her arms momentarily while, in a rush of confusion, random thoughts ran through her head. She didn't want to lead him on, and yet, it felt so comfortable to stand here in the darkened street wrapped in the warmth of his arms.

It was David who first broke the silence. "Do you think it would ever be possible for us?" He looked at her earnestly.

"I don't know, David." Lisl said. "I know I love you dearly as a friend, and anything more than that... well, I honestly haven't given it any thought." Her voice was soft in the warm night as she spoke into the quietness. "That's not to say that I couldn't or that it isn't possible," she continued. "It's just that there is someone in Vilseck-Grafenwöhr that has sort of won my heart."

"Why don't you tell me about him," David suggested as he drew her hand into the crook of his arm, and they continued their walk.

"He's an American. An officer. We've been dating rather casually for a short time now, but I just feel like there is so much there, at least, there is for me, anyway." She told him of Al and how they had met. Lisl looked up at David shyly. "Do you think I'm being foolish to hang my hopes on the slight chance that something more will come of this?"

"I don't know, Lisl. I'm hardly an expert in affairs of the heart. But I do know this: when your eyes light up each time you mention your American officer's name, you have to follow your heart." David gazed deep into her eyes, then smiled a sad, little smile. "Just remember, if this love of yours doesn't work out, you can always call me and I'll be there no matter what."

Lisl kissed him on the cheek and said, "You are a wonderful friend, and you will make some lucky girl a truly fine husband someday."

"I'm not so sure about that. I guess you can see, by my clumsy attempts at romance, that I'm hardly experienced enough to make anyone a husband right now. Besides, I need to make peace with the ghosts that still haunt me before I enter into any serious relationship."

"David, you need to talk about your experiences in Dachau as a first step in the healing process. You'll never be able to live with the past if you don't confront it first." Her words sounded right, and Lisl wondered where did she obtain all this wisdom? She didn't even know what experiences David was referring to. Yet, something told her, after reading the newspapers and hearing of all the concentration camp horrors that had been coming to light in the last year, that whatever David went through was of the most agonizing and heartbreaking experience.

They walked the rest of the way home in silence. Finally as

they reached the Wenzel's house, David pointed to the bench in the garden and said, "Maybe you're right. Let's sit out here a little and let me tell you what happened." He spoke quietly, his eyes reflecting a distant past that, even in the darkness, Lisl found eerie. "My parents, younger brother and I were taken from our apartment in Munich in November of '42 and sent to Dachau. We were told we were to be "resettled" — that was the word for it. All our belongings, our furniture, our money — it was all confiscated by the SS. When we arrived at the camp in Dachau, we were told to line up at the loading platform. My brother, along with some other children and a few elderly people, was pulled out of the line and was marched off to some buildings on the left. He was only thirteen, and I never saw him again. My mother became hysterical and was sent right away to the women's barracks. My father and I were placed on work details. My father was a pharmacist and so was assigned to the camp dispensary. I had a strong back so I was put on road construction duty. The work was hard, particularly when it snowed. We never had enough warm clothing nor enough food. In the men's barracks, we slept six to a bunk. They made us line up sardine-style, the bunks were so over-crowded. Eventually, typhus broke out and a clean-up squad came by every day to pick up the dead. Men were dropping like flies. If disease didn't get them, the back-breaking work did. We had so many strict regulations, and the slightest infraction of any of them got you a beating from the *kapos*."

"What were the *kapos*?" Lisl asked hesitantly.

David smiled. "They were one of us. They were Jews who had somehow ingratiated themselves to the Nazis, and were made guards. They were, of course, the most hated, more so than the SS because, as I said, they were from our ranks. They were also the ones who told us about the gas chambers and crematorium. Hundreds of Jews were taken from the barracks daily and herded to the death chambers. They were made to strip first before being jammed into the gas chambers. They were told it was a special shower for delousing and staying clean and free of disease, that they would all have to take this special shower. Well, after they were all killed, the bodies were carted by a special rail system to the crematorium for burning. I tell you, Lisl, the smokestacks from that crematorium burned day and night. We never knew which one of us would be next. Some of us refused to believe what was actually happening. I recall a bunkmate of mine — I don't remember his name — who said when he was called up as part of the next group to go, 'How do we know it isn't really a shower, Levine? They could be telling us the truth, you know.'" David paused a moment. "I guess we all have our way of maintaining our sanity. At any rate, I never saw him again.

"One day I went over to the dispensary with a feigned illness just so I could see my father and to see if he had any word about Mother. They were dismantling the dispensary after having stepped up their mass executions. I guess they felt there was no longer any need to waste medicine on people that were scheduled to die anyway. My father was nowhere in sight and after asking around, I found out that he had been taken to the gas chamber the day before. From that day on, I lost my will to live. I prayed that they *would* take me next so that I could escape from the misery and hell that I was living. The only thing that kept me going was the slight chance that my mother was still alive. I became obsessed with trying to find out how she was faring through a complicated message system at the camp. You know there was barbed wire everywhere — they even used it to block off individual barracks from each other. Anyway, through this complicated message system, I was able to learn that my mother had contracted typhus, but was still alive. At great risk to myself — but at that point, I didn't care — I was able to get a message to her to tell her that we all loved her and were just waiting for this war to end so that we can be together again as a family. She died shortly after receiving my message."

David looked at Lisl who was crying silently while listening to his story. He reached over and hugged her for a moment. After a while he continued, "Once my family was gone, life simply became a waiting game. I no longer felt the blows from the numerous beatings I received. I didn't care if they starved me, or worked me to death. I was numb, and I stayed that way until the American troops came to the camp in May of '45 and opened the gates. Many of the liberators cried when they saw us — those of us that had survived. Somehow, I'm still not sure how, I wandered out of the camp. The liberators had already set up a triage area, and the Red Cross was moving in as well, but somehow in my delirium, I wandered out determined to find my family. I knew I still had an aunt in Munich, and, I guess, I was determined to somehow get to her house. That's when you found me, Lisl, in that ditch by the side of the road. I had apparently passed out from hunger and dehydration. At any rate, that's the memory of this war that I will always carry with me. That and this number on my arm." He showed Lisl the blue numerals tattooed on the inside of his forearm.

"I'm so sorry — I'm so sorry," Lisl said through her tears. "It makes me so angry that these monsters who did this to you and your family were my countrymen. That they dared to call themselves German! David, you're a German just as much as I am. We're honorable people. What mutation, what fluke of nature would cause a whole group of people like these Nazis to perform unspeakable crimes against an entire race? It's beyond my comprehension." Lisl buried her face in her hands and cried bitter tears.

"Lisl. . . Lisl. . . it's beyond every decent human being's comprehension." David was stroking her hair as he spoke. "Unfortunately, we will have to live with these 'unspeakable crimes' as you put it, for a long, long time." They held each other as they both cried bitter tears of loss. Presently, they made a pact to always stay friends and to come to the aid of the other when needed. As the moon slowly floated out from behind a cloud, they parted ways, comfortable in the knowledge that their friendship was everlasting, and that they were both lucky to have found each other.

The months that followed found Lisl caught up in a whirlwind romance with Al Daughtery. The two were virtually inseparable. They quickly realized that they were made for each other. In spite of their different backgrounds, they surprisingly had much in common. They had the same likes and dislikes, yet when it came to strengths and weaknesses, they were a dichotomy of each other, almost a mirror image of each other, so that where Al was weak, Lisl was strong. Where Lisl came up short, Al's strength filled in. They were two pieces of a puzzle and, once put together, they joined perfectly in a seamless fit.

Throughout their courtship Lisl somehow felt that things were moving a little too fast. She was making a severe adjustment to the changes in her life. The war had been horrific — she mourned for all the countless lives that had been lost. The war trials in Nürnberg had been publicized for months; and, although, her country was being severely penalized with tariffs and heavy reparations, she felt victimized by the historic devastation. As a German country girl, Lisl had no more control over her fate than those who fought on the battlefields. She was fortunate to be a survivor, most definitely, but a survivor with deep scars. In spite of her doubts and concerns, she was desperately trying to get on with her life.

On more than one occasion, Lisl and Al would have long soul-searching conversations where they mused over the turn of events. One evening, after a particularly enjoyable dinner at a cozy local *Gasthaus*, Al pushed back his chair from the table, patted his stomach and said, "One thing I got to say about Germans — they sure know how to cook!"

"I would hope you could say more about us than that!" Lisl admonished.

The rosy light from the nearby fireplace glittered in his eyes and tinged his cheeks pink. "You're still disturbed over the black mark on your country that Hitler has left behind as his legacy?" he asked gently.

"Well, yes — yes, I am. You don't understand how cheated we feel — not out of a victory in this God-forsaken war — but of our honor, our pride in our country!" she said vehemently. "In order to understand our feelings," she continued, "you have to go back many centuries. First, the Germans always have been a proud people. They have always been self-reliant and industrious. After World War I, we were stripped of our pride and our dignity. The United States passed the Smoot-Hawley Act in 1930 levying stiff tariffs against us that we couldn't even begin to pay! Our economy became a shamble. Banks collapsed like a house of cards, and unemployment reached an all-time high. My oldest sister had just married, and overnight all of her life savings became worthless. She and her husband had thousands of marks in the bank one day and nothing but the clothes on their backs the next.

"That's when Hitler came along. At the same time the United States refused to join the League of Nations, choosing instead to adopt its isolationist policy. Hitler offered us jobs, security, a stable economy — everything we so desperately needed at the time. But in the end, he betrayed all of us — the German people included. The worst betrayal of all was the anti-Semitism that came with his dictatorship. To me, that will be the stain on my country that may never go away. Not that the persecution of Jews was ever a uniquely German thing — just look at the Inquisition in Spain. They burned thousands of Jews and took away their children to be raised as Christians. And what about the pogroms against Jews in the ghettoes of Russia or Poland? I'm not suggesting that any of it was remotely tolerable nor am I trying to diminish the seriousness of what happened. I'm only saying what the Nazis did was the tragic outcome of a fanatical leader gone mad — not the results of the efforts of the German citizenry." Lisl paused to catch her breath and was suddenly aware that she had never voiced her concerns openly like this before. Al was leaning forward listening intently.

"What most people, particularly the English and Americans, don't realize is that Hitler held us under his thumb, also. We weren't all Nazis, you know. We're Germans — the terms are not interchangeable!" she said. "We feared and hated Hitler's Nazis as much as anyone. Unfortunately, we were the ones under their rule — their power, and *we* were duped, also. Which is why we welcomed the Americans so much when they took over our town. We felt liberated from the terrible dictatorship that had held us in its grip too long."

Al listened soberly and after a pause, said, "It's times like this when I see your eyes blazing that I want to take you in my arms and protect you. I don't ever want you to feel the pain, the bigotry and prejudices of people who will never know what you went through."

Lisl took his hand and said quietly, "Because of what is now coming to light and everything that the Nazis did during the war, I feel that I will always go through life with a sense of shame and humiliation — to be labeled as a member of a race whose crimes against humanity were an outrage to civilized societies everywhere. Think of it, Al, millions of Jews — men, women and children — slaughtered in those concentration camps. Horror heaped upon horror. Unspeakable atrocities — I and people like me had nothing to do with any of it. Yet, we are the ones who bear the guilt. Will this burden of guilt ever end? Will the stain ever be washed away?" It was a question she would ask herself many times throughout her life.

Al lit a cigarette and watched her quietly through the blue haze.

Lisl looked up at him and said, "I just need to adjust, and I need to do it in my own time."

During the next few weeks, Al wooed her with gifts, flowers and countless enchanted evenings; glamorous trips to a nearby ski resort, Garmisch-Partenkirchen where they enjoyed colorful Ice Capades shows at the famous Casa Carioca nightclub. The ice show was like no other floor show Lisl had seen before. The ice was frozen in the design of a huge American flag surrounded by thousands of silk flowers embedded in the ice, their fresh-like beauty captured forever.

After the show, the ice was rolled back to reveal a hardwood dance floor where they kicked up their heels and jitterbugged to "In The Mood," "String of Pearls," and all the familiar hits of the '40s.

They took long walks in the park together, they dined in little out-of-the way restaurants. And, all the while, Al continually referred to the time when they would be married.

"I don't know about you, but I want us to have lots of children," he remarked as they strolled home hand-in-hand one evening. The lushness of summer was evident in the soft, green leaves on the trees, and the birds that sang joyously. "I only had one brother and one sister, and I know you have three sisters, but I'd like for us to have at least five or six kids. What do you think? And when we move Stateside," he went on without waiting for her reply, "we'll buy a big house somewhere out in the country. Maybe a little patch of land we could work. Since my parents never had any real land to speak of, it's always been my dream to own as much acreage as I can afford."

Lisl felt a slight sense of uneasiness overcome her briefly. She had had enough of farm life while growing up and was just starting to enjoy the pleasures of city living. She recalled those golden summers in Munich when, as a child, she'd visit her oldest sister Maria in her elegant townhouse. How she loved the hustle and bustle of city dwelling. "Aren't you rushing things a bit, Al?" she replied lightly.

"Why not rush? I know I'm crazy about you. And you feel the same way about me, or, at least, I thought you did. . ."

"I do, I do," she reassured him. "It's just that our backgrounds are so vastly different, our cultures. . ." Her voice trailed off as she struggled to find the right words. How could she make him understand? She didn't want him to just take it for granted that they would marry. She wanted him to ask her, not just assume and make plans like how many children they would have. She realized that Al, being an officer, was a take-charge kind of man, but, it was important for her to be included in the decision-making process that would affect their lives together. Five or six children? She hadn't even given any thought to having any children yet! "What I'm trying to say, Al, is let me get used to the idea of dating someone like you first, before we start planning any children. You're the only man I've ever dated, you know."

"Is that what it is? Do you want to go out with other guys for a while? Because if it is, then, fine. You can just go find someone else!" he said angrily.

"Al, that's not what I mean," she replied miserably. This was not turning out at all like she wanted.

They walked along in silence. As they approached her apartment, Al took her hand and said, "Look, I thought we were so right for each other. I didn't know you'd have these doubts."

"I'm not even sure they're doubts. I think I just want to enjoy dating someone for a while. . . without thinking about the future. I want to be carefree for a while, can't you understand that? After everything that's happened to me with the war and all. . . I don't know. . ." Lisl brushed her eyes with the back of her hand and looked off in the distance.

"Okay," Al conceded, "maybe I *have* rushed things with you a bit. How about we just not see each other for a while as sort of a test period? If we're truly right for each other, we'll both know it. If not, we'll know that soon enough as well."

Lisl lifted her face to him and her eyes glistened with tears. "Maybe that would be the best, if that's what you want," she whispered hoarsely.

"Honey, it's not what *I* want," his voice was tinged with exasperation. "It's the only solution to our problem. If you're not sure now, this is the only way we can both be sure. He caught her fingertips and kissed them. "Look, I'll call you six weeks from now, and we'll see how we feel about each other at that time, okay?"

She nodded numbly. Her heart felt like lead as she slowly let herself into the apartment. Thankfully, Trudi was already asleep. Lisl was not up to explaining her tears right now. All she wanted to do was draw a hot bath and then go to bed.

Once out of the tub, she sat at her dressing table and stared at her reflection in the mirror. Had he really wanted her? Why her? With his incredible good looks, Al could have any woman he wanted. And there were certainly plenty of them on the post. Good-looking women, too. Lisl had admired the self-assured way the young American women she saw every day carried themselves. Their blue jeans with the rolled up cuffs, their saddle-oxfords and bobby socks, the way their shiny ponytails bounced when they walked. These were the women Al ought to be with. Yet, he had wanted her even though their lives were worlds apart. The alarm clock ticked a steady beat as she sat lost in her thoughts. She was tired and confused. There was no point in trying to figure it all out tonight. After all, she had six weeks to do that — six long weeks. Had she done the right thing in voicing her concern? Had she made a mistake by speaking up? Of course not! It was *his* problem for reacting so sensitively. She had had so many heartaches in her young life that now she wanted to exercise some sort of control over her destiny. Was that so wrong? Why couldn't Al just not be so sure of everything? Why couldn't she be *more* sure of things! Oh, it was far more than she could deal with tonight. Her emotions and fatigue overcame her, and she softly cried herself to sleep.

She couldn't eat. She couldn't sleep. She fought spells of nausea and headaches. She showed up at work, red-eyed and subdued. Trudi, true friend that she was, tried to help, but it was futile. On a wet, dreary morning after two weeks, Lisl sat down, markedly thinner, to the soft-boiled egg and toast that Trudi had prepared for her. "You've been such a good roommate, Trudi, to help me through all this," she said gratefully.

"Well, I've been thinking, and I think I know what would do you a lot of good," Trudi smiled her mischievous smile.

"What?" Lisl asked glumly.

"Let's go home this weekend. It'll do you good to see your parents again."

"We'll go if you want to, but nothing is going to help," Lisl replied miserably.

"Lisl! This is getting ridiculous! Why don't you just call Al and tell him you've thought it over and you want to go back with him?" Trudi asked.

Lisl was horrified. "Are you crazy? I can't ever do that. A girl doesn't just call a man to tell him that!"

"Oh, heavens to Betsy! Whoever made up such ridiculous rules, anyway? Probably a man. I say, if you've got something to say, say it. It shouldn't matter what gender you are," Trudi retorted, her hands on her hips.

Lisl wished she could be more like Trudi. Although not beautiful in the true sense of the word, her dark-haired friend was always sure of what she wanted and always got what she wanted. With eyes sparkling with intelligence and mischief, Trudi was so strong, so bursting with life. She had her pick of boyfriends. She charmed each one equally and convinced each man she met that he was the most wonderful man in the world and could do no wrong. Consequently, they beat a path to her door.

"Nevertheless," Lisl said, "I can't call him. I'll just have to wait four more weeks and hope that he still wants me."

"Of course, he'll still want you. In the meantime, let's go to Altmannstein. It'll be fun!"

Lisl's thoughts turned to David. She wondered if he was still in

Altmannstein or if, perhaps, he had gone back to school as he had intended. Maybe he's found someone else by now. He certainly deserved someone good. Someone true, someone who'll love him with all her heart, because that was what her friend deserved. Fresh tears welled up inside her again. Will the tears ever stop? she thought bitterly.

Altmannstein proved to be the elixir Trudi had promised. Lisl's parents were overjoyed to see them. Home was such a comforting place to be. She could almost forget Al here, at least for a little while. David, her father told her, had gone on to Heidelberg to continue his studies. He promised to write regularly, Michael said, and, oh, yes, he asked about Lisl, wanting to know if she found happiness with her American officer.

Lisl lowered her eyes, not wanting to meet her father's inquisitive gaze. "Father, right now, I'm not seeing anyone. Al and I have agreed to stay apart for a while because we want to be sure we're totally right for each other before we make any permanent plans together," she said in a low voice. She hoped she could stay in control long enough for the explanation to suffice.

Michael lit his pipe and blew out the match before answering. He puffed thoughtfully and replied, "I think that may be a very wise idea, Lisl. Whatever comes of this, you know, will be for the best, one way or the other."

She threw her father a grateful look as her mother called for her from the kitchen. She could always count on Father to help put things in their proper perspective.

"Do you need some help, Mama?" she asked as she put her arm around her mother's shoulders. How frail she's becoming, Lisl thought with alarm. It seemed in the few short months Lisl had been away from home, her parents had shrunk noticeably. Not only that, her room seemed much tinier than she remembered it being. How can everything seem so much smaller just because one has been away for a while?

As the weekend drew to a close, Michael loaded Trudi's car to the gills once more with food, and with a flurry of good-byes, the two girls headed back to Vilseck-Grafenwöhr.

The days seemed to drag on endlessly. Lisl went through the motions of everyday living. She worked, she ate what little she could, she slept when she could, she went out with friends, but only at Trudi's insistence. All the while, she wondered what Al was doing at the moment. Was he thinking of her right now? Was he pining away as she was? Or, she thought darkly, was he dating someone new? Perhaps, he has forgotten all about her and was now madly in love with a perky American girl. Lisl knew she was torturing herself like this, but she couldn't help it. She was miserable. She spent many evenings alone in her darkened room listening to the little radio on her bedside table. The melancholy strains of "Star Dust" drifted on the darkness.

Sometimes I wonder why I spend the lonely night
Dreaming of a song? The melody haunts my reverie,
And I am once again with you
When our love was new and each kiss an inspiration...

Shaking her head, Lisl knew this was all wrong. She mustn't torment herself like this. Yet, her heart was heavy with grief and longing. She longed for Al's touch, the warmth of his smile, the comfort of his arms. How much more of this could she take?

Finally, six weeks to the day of their break up, the phone downstairs rang and *Frau* Apfel came to the door. "There's a phone call for Lisl," she said as Trudi opened the door. The older woman's face was all smiles and her eyes twinkled with delight. Without hesitating Lisl bolted past both of them and ran down the stairs.

"Hello?" she answered breathlessly.

There was a momentary pause at the other end of the line, and then, "I can't get you out of my mind," he said.

Lisl basked in the rich, resonant voice and suddenly pure happiness drenched her entire being, making her weak at the knees. She found her own voice and replied. "I feel the same way, Al."

"Have you been as miserable as I have?" he asked quietly.

"More, I'm sure," she murmured.

He continued, "I haven't been able to eat or sleep..."

Violins played symphonies in her head; the world smelled of a thousand roses; a hundred dancers danced around her, and tears of relief streamed down her face as she listened to his woeful litany of heartache. They made plans to meet the next night and decide what to do.

"I've got to find something really special to wear this time," Lisl mused as she stood in front of her closet.

Trudi burst out laughing. "What a change has come over you. I'm so glad to see that you're not moping around here anymore!"

Lisl shot her friend an affectionate glance. "You were such a dear to help me these last few weeks."

"Wear that tailored pink linen dress with the matching bolero jacket. Since you've lost so much weight, it's probably the only thing that will still fit you," Trudi suggested.

Trudi was right. The dress fit perfectly, clinging to all the right places, but still projecting an elegant look with the fine tailored design. The tiny black polka dots of the dress were offset with Lisl's smart black patent leather pumps and matching wide patent leather belt. She brushed her hair until it shone, then pinned it in a smooth, sophisticated upsweep.

Al picked her up at seven sharp, once again admiring her choice of clothing. "You've lost weight, haven't you?" he asked suspiciously.

"Not that much," Lisl replied nonchalantly.

"Yes, you have. Why, look," he said as his hands encircled her trim waist, "my fingers almost touch, your waist is so tiny."

"That's just because you have such big hands, you big lug," she laughed.

"God, it's good to see you again," he said as he wrapped his arms around her and buried his face in her hair.

The floor show was spectacular, as usual, and both of them thoroughly enjoyed themselves. Afterwards, Al was peculiarly subdued as they drove home in silence. The only sound was the slap-slap of the windshield wipers' futile attempt at wiping the sheets of rain from the glass.

"I had a good time tonight," Lisl offered as she snuggled up to him in the car.

"I did, too, Honey."

"Is anything wrong? You're awfully quiet," she asked.

They pulled into the front drive of her apartment building. Al turned off the engine and turned to look at her.

"Lisl, I've been thinking. . . I don't want to go through again what we went through these last few weeks. I know now that I want to spend the rest of my life with you. Do you want to spend the rest of your life with me?"

"Why, Lieutenant, is that a marriage proposal?" Lisl asked gently.

"Yes, it is. Let me put it another way: Will you marry me?" This time he waited for a reply. He held her intently by the shoulders while searching her face for an answer.

Lisl looked up at the man she loved. The love and tenderness in his eyes were overwhelming.

"Yes — oh, yes, yes!" she cried.

Suddenly she was caught up in a crushing bear hug as Al whooped with joy.

"We can get married right away," he went on. "It'll take some time to get the paperwork in order. The Army frowns on marriages with our former enemies — but, what the hell. Just let them try to keep us apart!" He looked at her with a broad grin.

"So fast, so soon. Oh, Al, are you sure? I wouldn't want to get you in trouble with your superiors," Lisl said.

"No problem. A lot of my buddies have German war brides. It's just a little paperwork; no big deal, really. The only thing that's restricted is that post privileges are denied to German war brides. Leave it to me to choose a former enemy as my bride," he smiled ruefully. "If you had been Italian or French, you could use the commissary and PX or anything else on the post."

A hurt look came over Lisl's face as old doubts came back momentarily. "Well, maybe, you should find yourself someone more suitable," she said quietly.

"Sweetheart. . . I'd never have it any other way," he replied, the love shining in his eyes. "I could easily live without that if it meant having you as my wife. Of course, I'll need to ask your father for your hand. I want to do this the proper way, you know."

Lisl's heart swelled with tenderness. "You'll have no problem with Father. He's already very fond of you."

"I don't know," Al said, eyeing her skeptically, "you're pretty special to him. Any fool can see that."

"Well, if he protests too much," Lisl laughed, "Mama and I will just have to convince him that you're the man for me!"

Lisl suppressed a giggle as Al wrapped his arms around her and nuzzled her neck.

"I was so afraid you might not have me," he said after a while.

"Not have you? Why on earth not?" Lisl asked as she gently stroked his cheek with the back of her fingers.

He gathered her up in his arms as they snuggled together in the car. "Well, now is as good a time as any to tell you, I suppose," he started.

Oh, no. What horrible thing did he have to confess to her now? Lisl thought with dread. Perhaps he's been married before; maybe has children somewhere. That wouldn't be so bad. Lisl couldn't imagine what terrible things he was about to divulge to her.

"I was in the war for a long time. I fought on almost every major front including Italy, France. . . I was even in the Battle of the Bulge. The things I saw and the things I had to do were barbaric. If you only knew. . . I'm a monster really." His voice grew husky.

Lisl looked up at him and started to say something, but he quickly placed a finger over her lips and said, "No, no, let me finish. I have to tell you everything while I have the nerve, or else it won't be fair to you. I want you to make an informed decision about marrying me. I want you to know exactly what you're getting. And, if. . ." he hesitated. ". . . if you decide to change your mind about marrying me, I'll certainly understand.

"I was a newly commissioned second lieutenant assigned to the Third Army led by General Patton. I saw action in Italy, France, Belgium as well as Germany. Patton pushed us unbelievably. Sometimes in our marches we covered sixty-five miles a day in order to re-capture a city that the Germans had just occupied. I fought at Verdun, France, which was a major keystone of the Maginot Line; we fought Il Duce's Fascists in Palermo, Italy. I won't bore you with all the details of every battle, but I just want you to know that in all these battles I killed a lot of men. . . personally, I mean. Lisl, if you knew some of the things my men and I did, I'm not sure you'd want to marry me. I'm a monster, you know. I was trained to be a killing monster and that's what I became."

Lisl looked up at his face and was shocked to see tears streaming down his cheeks as he spoke.

"Sometimes, even to this day, I wake up in the middle of the night, and I'm drenched in a cold sweat. Loud noises still make me flinch. If I think about some of my experiences too much, my hands start shaking. One time while we were in battle, I shot an advancing Nazi soldier that had somehow broken through the line and was within six feet of me. I shot him in the head point blank. The top of his head simply disappeared, and when I looked down at my map there was brain tissue all over it. I didn't have time to think about what had just happened. I just brushed off the map and carried on. It wasn't until much later that I reacted. I went into the latrine and threw up my guts. It wasn't the blood and gore that got to me, don't you understand? It was the fact that a human life could be snuffed out in an instant in such a horrible way. That man probably had a family, a mother, a wife, kids... and in only an instant he was a lump of meat left to rot on a battlefield."

Lisl listened quietly. Thoughts of Stefan haunted her. Al was echoing the same words Stefan had felt, and her heart ached for both men who had been caught up in the senseless destruction of war.

How could she offer comfort to this man so racked by grief, by guilt? Would his soul ever heal completely? Lisl doubted it. "Al," she began gently, "every intelligent human being that ever took part in a war must have these thoughts. The trick, I guess, is to deal with them, live with them, and try to go on. You have to deal with your experiences just as I have to deal with mine. Granted, you have far more demons to fight than I do, but we each have an emotional battle nevertheless. Life does go on, Al. You had to do what you were trained to... what you were ordered to do. We all had to do what we were ordered to do. Everybody knows that in war all sense of reason and logic are suspended. The world is turned upside down. We're all wounded, damaged by war — we're all victims."

They sat quietly each lost in their own thoughts. After a while

Lisl added, "Let's help each other with our demons. We need to put the past behind us and think about our future together."

"Does this mean you still want to marry me?"

"I would be honored to be your wife," she smiled.

With a shaky sigh of relief Al wrapped his arms around her and held her tight.

"Everything's going to be okay," she soothed, "it's going to be okay."

That following Sunday morning, Al and Lisl drove to Altmannstein. The sky was crystalline clear and bright. The couple held hands and sat in comfortable silence while the radio played softly. Every now and then Al cleared his throat as he wondered how he would approach Lisl's father. Al was certainly fond of the old man even though he was hard to read — those steel-blue eyes that seemed to penetrate right through Al as if to say, "What do you want with my daughter?" It was easy to see he was crazy about his youngest, and that was what was going to be the hardest to overcome. Could Al do it? Could he, an American, overcome the barriers, not the least of which is the language barrier, to convince this staunch old German that he wanted to marry his daughter? The prospect of it brought tiny beads of sweat to Al's brow.

As if reading his thoughts, Lisl stroked the back of his neck and soothed, "Don't worry, you'll do fine with Father. I've already told him and Mama how wonderful you are and how much I love you. So, you see, I've already prepared the way for you." Her eyes danced with merriment.

"Easy for you to say — you don't have to stumble all over yourself with a language you can't understand!"

Lisl exploded with peals of laughter. "If you only knew. . . If you only knew!"

" But," she said after regaining her composure, "you needn't worry as long as you learn a few phrases. Just make the effort. You don't know how much they appreciate it when you make an effort to learn their language." She turned to face him. "Here try this: *'Ich möchte Ihre Tochter heiraten'* Or, better yet, try this: *'Darf ich Ihre Tochter heiraten?'* "

Al glanced at her uneasily. "Darf eeck earie. . .I can't do it!" he said with a resigning sigh.

"Yes, you can. I know you can do it. It's not that hard. Now try it again: *'Darf ich Ihre. . .'* " And so, they continued, as they sped along the Autobahn towards the little town of Altmannstein.

As they slowly drove into town and up the steep hill to Lisl's parents house, neighborhood children ran alongside of them in gleeful welcome. The shiny American car was a novelty in the ancient village, and Lisl was proud to be riding in it, if not driving it.

"They're here, Father!" Maria cried as she ran out to greet them, arms outstretched ready to embrace both Lisl and Al at the same time. "Come into the house — I hope you both are hungry. We have so much food prepared, and we can't save any of it!"

"You better eat a lot," Lisl said under her breath as she leaned toward Al, "that'll help you score points, at least with Mama."

"I need all the help I can get," Al whispered back as they entered the living room.

The meal, as always, was excellent. Al duly stuffed himself with pork chops, sliced potatoes, blue cabbage and gravy. Later Maria brought out a crisp golden apple strudel still warm from the oven. While Lisl helped her mother clear the dishes, Michael and Al went outside to sit on the bench and enjoy a couple of cigars together in the cool evening air.

I'm sure he knows why I want to talk to him, thought Al as he listened to Michael talk. The older man had been telling him a little about the history of Altmannstein in an effort to put the nervous young American at ease. "Sir, I'm sure you know why I'm here today," Al began, "I love your daughter very much," he glanced over at Michael as he spoke. The cool, pale eyes regarded him calmly. "Lisl has become the light of my life, and it would be an honor if you would give me her hand in marriage. *Darf ich Ihre Tochter heiraten?*" There — he's said it. Al waited nervously for Michael's reply. Slowly the warmth crept into the eyes, a smile played at the corners of the lips, and then, "If I have your word as an officer and a gentleman that you will cherish and love her forever as I have her mother, then I would be proud to have you as my son-in-law."

Lisl wondered how it was going outside and thought several times of checking. No, she decided, Al is a big boy; he will have to handle this himself. Men always somehow manage to iron these delicate things out amongst themselves anyway. It was best to let Al and her father bond with each other without any interference from her.

Just as the last cup was dried and put up in the cupboard, Al and Michael came walking into the living room, their arms around each other's shoulders.

"Mama, break out the Schnapps!" Michael announced. "We must celebrate our daughter's betrothal. Lisl and Al are getting married!"

And so it was, in October of 1946 after the military paperwork was completed, Lisl and Al were married.

CHAPTER 12

European society of the times dictated that when a couple married, they had two weddings: one a civil ceremony performed at the city hall for civilian record, and the second, a religious service in a church. The second wasn't nearly as important as the first.

Lisl stood before her closet that October morning carefully selecting a well-tailored navy blue wool suit. Its jacket had broad shoulders and a nipped-in waist that showed off the slender figure her soon-to-be-husband was so proud of. The matching skirt flared softly at the knees. A simple, singular strand of pearls with matching earrings completed the ensemble. Al picked her up in his brand new 1946 baby blue Oldsmobile.

"I can't believe we're actually getting married," she said sliding in on the passenger's side as he held the door open for her. He smiled tenderly at her and kissed the top of her nose.

Soon they were at the *Rathaus,* the German city hall. They were ushered into a large chamber with a high vaulted ceiling. Here the couple was met by a pallid, bespectacled clerk who took their papers and stamped them with an official-looking seal. After the two exchanged a few solemn words that echoed in the stillness, they took turns signing a huge, old-fashioned ledger, had their picture taken by a staff photographer and, before they knew it, they were Lieutenant and Mrs. Alvin Daughtery.

Holding hands, they emerged once again out into the dazzling sunlight. Hesitating only briefly, the couple gleefully ran down the stone steps of city hall like two children suddenly released from school.

The next day they were married again in the religious ceremony: this time in the post chapel. Lisl's friend Trudi and one of Al's buddies, a lieutenant from Indiana stood up for them. The post chaplain was a kind, soft-spoken man who frequently patted Lisl's hand in reassurance when he saw how nervous she was. Although her parents had been able to come, Lisl sorely missed all her friends being present. Lisl and Al had decided to downplay the ceremony, keeping it quick and low-key. Lisl's wedding dress was a simple but elegant cream-colored suit — certainly not the elaborate lace and tulle concoction her sisters wore at their nuptials, but Lisl felt like a bride nevertheless. She carried a small bouquet of peach carnations and hothouse lilies-of-the-valley as she took her father's arm to walk down the aisle. It had been a gloomy, rainy day, unlike the day before, when suddenly the clouds opened up, and, as the couple exchanged vows, sharp rays of sunlight poured in through the high, stained glass windows of the chapel . Lisl took that as a good omen. Perhaps, she thought, if their marriage was not entirely blessed by the U.S. Army, certainly the Lord was smiling down on them. She silently promised herself that she would be the loving, devoted wife that a wonderful man such as Al deserved.

The couple lived off-post in the same neighborhood where Trudi and Lisl had lived. She continued to work as an overseas switchboard operator in order to supplement Al's pay and save for the future.

To understand their economic situation of the times, one has to examine the events taking place at the time. It is well known that after any war, to the victor go the spoils. In the case of post-war Germany however, the defeated country was divided into four zones occupied by the four victorious powers, the U. S., Great Britain, France, and the U.S.S. R. The Allies were intent on achieving political decentralization, the dismantling of German war industries and reparation. Instead, they found themselves faced with a quite different set of problems: economic stagnation, famine, a rampant black market, and, most importantly, an unstable currency. This coupled with fundamental differences between the occupying powers themselves, namely the breakdown of the alliance between the U. S. and Great Britain on the one side and the U. S. S. R. on the other, produced continual conflict and confusion. Prolonged negotiations, beginning with the Potsdam Agreement in the summer of 1945 and lasting well into 1948, took its toll in the further demoralization of the German people who were desperately trying to rebuild their lives after the devastating war.

Clearly a comprehensive plan for reorganization was needed. The turning point in the postwar history of Lisl's country was the year 1948, when several drastic changes in the German government occurred. One was the expansion of the newly formed German Economic Council for the combined British and American bi-zone and a much-needed nationwide currency reform which was put into operation on June 20. Overnight, all German citizens became economic equals — those who had been relatively wealthy with the inflated *Deutschmark* and those who had nothing woke up the morning of June 21 on the same economic footing. To help out its struggling citizens, the infant *Landtage* or state parliament, implemented a headstart program which provided each person with eighty marks to aid in economic recovery.

As a German war bride, Lisl was not allowed to use the American commissary. Consequently, she and Al had to live off the German economy and suffer through the currency reform that ultimately led to a remarkable economic recovery for the country in general. Furthermore, they knew that Al would eventually be transferred back to the States, and so they felt they could endure for the time being, and look forward to better times and a long, happy life together.

Also in 1948, Al's tour of duty in Germany was up. However, Lisl's father fell ill and was diagnosed as having stomach cancer. Lisl quickly applied for a leave of absence and soon divided her time between Vilseck-Grafenwöhr and Altmannstein.

"Honey, you look exhausted," Al said to her one evening as she was unpacking from one of her many trips to Altmannstein. She had just learned to drive and soon discovered that the Autobahn was no place for a novice driver.

"I don't know how long I can keep this up. Father needs surgery, and he needs me by his side. You're about to get your papers and, I suppose, we'll be leaving for the States. I just feel so torn. . ."

Al took her in his arms and said," Well, maybe you'll be glad to hear what I have to tell you, my lovely bride." After two years of marriage, Al still called her his bride.

"What is it?" Lisl asked through her tears.

"I've re-upped here at the post, and we're staying in Germany for three more years."

"Oh, Al! Do you mean that?" Lisl asked incredulously.

"Yeah, I knew you needed to stay here for your father, and I certainly didn't want to leave without you, so here we are. The only change is that we *are* being transferred. To Landshut, the Army post there is bigger, and, if you want to continue working there, you can."

Lisl hugged her husband fiercely and said, "You're so wonderful. Thank you for being so understanding."

Fortunately, her father's cancer went into remission, and she and Al moved to a more spacious apartment in Landshut. Going back to work was no longer an issue for in September, Lisl discovered they were expecting a baby.

The spring of 1949 was a relatively peaceful and happy time for Lisl and Al. Landshut was a beautiful, historic old city, and the young wife delighted in her routine of shopping and fixing up the two-bedroom apartment Al had found for them. They had painted the apartment together, and Lisl took great pains in sewing all the curtains throughout their home. Nearing the end of her pregnancy, she waddled into the nursery one sunny morning in May to show Trudi the handcrafted bassinet that Al had refinished over the winter.

"My! You have everything ready, and it all looks so neat and tidy. Wait till the baby comes — it won't be so neat and tidy then," she chided. Although now married herself, Trudi had taken the time to visit with her that day while Al was at work.

"Well, you know how organized I've always been. After all, we've had nine months to get ready for the big event," Lisl laughed.

They stood together in the bright, cheery room filled with yellow sunshine. Suddenly Lisl felt a strange sensation as a gush of warm water ran down her legs and splashed on the hardwood floor.

She stood there for a moment and stared at the puddle. Trudi's mouth dropped open. "Oh, my God!"

Just then a cramping pain tore through Lisl's lower back and abdomen. She instinctively wrapped her arms around her belly and sat down.

"Lisl, we need to get you to the hospital."

Lisl looked up and Trudi's face had gone white.

"There's no time," Lisl said, grimacing, "Call *Frau* Wengenroth from downstairs, her sister is a midwife. Maybe she can come right away."

Lisl felt a sudden surge of excitement as she realized she would soon be a mother. At that moment, another pain seized the lower half of her body so brutally she had to put her hand to her mouth to keep from screaming. "Oh, Trudi, Trudi. . . I think. . .the baby's coming right now!" The pains were far more severe at this early stage than she was prepared for, and she desperately hoped the midwife would come in time. Between contractions, Trudi helped her to the bed, then ran downstairs to fetch help.

An hour later the midwife came to find Lisl well into advanced labor, her face streaming with sweat, and her hair plastered around her face in damp ringlets. She clutched Trudi's hand tightly as she fought to catch her breath for another contraction.

Sizing up the situation quickly, the midwife expertly proceeded to check her vital signs, drape her with clean sheets, and place pillows under her knees, all the while, intoning her words of comfort, "You're doing just fine, Lisl. Soon it'll all be over, and you'll have a fine, healthy baby. Won't that be nice?"

Lisl answered her with a long, animal-like moan. By then she was instinctively pushing with all her might.

Trudi shouted with excitement, "Keep pushing, Lisl, I see the baby's head!"

The room swam in front of her as she rode the crest of pain with one more monumental push.

"Good. . . good," the midwife soothed as she took the crowning baby that was presenting itself to the world. She quickly wrapped it in a clean towel and wiped the baby's face and mouth. Lisl closed her eyes and listened to the tiny mewling that quickly turned into a strong, lusty cry.

"You have a healthy baby girl, my dear," said the beaming midwife.

Lisl looked up and saw tears in Trudi's eyes. "She's beautiful, Lisl."

"Where's Al? Has anybody gone to get him?" she asked weakly as the midwife placed the swaddled baby next to her.

"He's on his way," Trudi answered.

Lisl cradled her daughter and marveled at the perfection of this newborn child. The baby gazed up at her, her little pink mouth opened and formed a perfect "O."

Trudi helped the midwife finish up, then put the baby in her new bassinet while Lisl slept, totally exhausted.

They named their baby daughter Anita. Al invited what seemed like the entire post up to their apartment to view what he called "the most gorgeous baby on earth." Lisl's sister Maria came from Munich to help with all the extra chores that come with the care of a newborn.

"You've held her long enough, Al," Maria commanded as she walked into the nursery one day. "It's my turn to hold her."

"No — no, it's still my turn," said the petulant new father. "You can hold her all day while I'm at work — I can't."

He cradled the baby tenderly in his arms as he cooed softly, "I will bring the world to your feet, Anita, child of my heart. You'll have everything you will ever want, I'll see to that."

The baby looked up at him as if mesmerized by the lull of the words he spoke. She reached up and curled her tiny hand around his finger.

Maria put her hands on her hips and clucked, "You'll spoil her for sure with all that attention."

"I don't care," he said, smiling at the baby. "Just look at her, Maria. Isn't she beautiful? Look at those big, brown eyes. She looks just like me, doesn't she?"

"Yes," Maria said for the hundredth time, "she looks just like you. Now let me have her before your little Miss America spits up all over your uniform."

Al reluctantly handed the baby to Maria as Lisl wandered into the room.

"You two still fighting over that child?" she chided them.

"This weekend we're going home to Altmannstein to visit the folks and show off our brand new baby girl!" Al proudly announced.

"Are you sure we should, Al? She's only three weeks old."

"Of course we can," he assured her, "we'll just pack up her diapers and off we'll go — she'll be just fine."

True to his word, the following weekend they packed up the Oldsmobile and headed for Altmannstein. As they drove along the Autobahn, they stopped at the American Snackbar in Ingolstadt for a cup of coffee and a doughnut.

Al watched Lisl as she ate her doughnut while balancing the bundled baby on her lap.

"This reminds me of when we first met — that Christmas Eve in '45. I swept you off your feet with coffee and doughnuts."

"And you're still sweeping me off my feet, Captain Daughtery," Lisl smiled, "Only this time there are two of us to handle. Isn't that right, Sweetie?" she said to the baby. "Daddy has his hands full with us."

Anita gurgled with delight as she gazed up at her mother.

Soon they were back on the road again. Lisl sighed with contentment as she took in the rolling hills around them. It was June in Bavaria, and the flowers were in full bloom. The ugly remnants of war were long gone and everything seemed new again. Doris Day was softly crooning "Night and Day" on the radio.

As they drove up the narrow cobblestone road that led to her parent's house, Lisl could hardly contain her excitement. The proud grandparents were sitting outside in the garden eagerly awaiting their arrival.

"Imagine, Father," Maria said as she came towards them, "a granddaughter from our baby girl."

She held out her arms, and Lisl presented Anita to her. Michael came up behind her and looked at the baby. When he looked up, he had tears in his eyes.

"She's beautiful," he murmured. "She looks a lot like you, Al," Michael said in German. Lisl quickly translated for Al, and he beamed with pride.

"But she has Lisl's fair skin," Maria added, "which will really offset those dark eyes." Having settled the issue of the baby's looks, they all laughed and went inside.

Weekend trips home like this were always wonderful. Lisl's father had a keg of beer ready; her sisters and their husbands often joined them for an evening of food, fun and convivial merriment. Al and his father-in-law got along well in spite of the language barrier. Michael and Maria were pleased that this tall, strapping American could make their youngest daughter so happy. It was comical to see Al duck his head each time he entered the living room of Lisl's parent's home because he was so much taller than the door frame.

Naturally they never left empty-handed. Michael continued to load the trunk of their car with bags of apples, field-grown potatoes, bacon and canned goods from Maria's well-stocked larder.

On more than one occasion, Lisl took Al up into the hills with her to experience the joy and deep inner peace that never failed to overcome her each time she set foot on those majestic hills high above the town of her birth. Al was her life and these hills were her foundation, and somehow she wanted the two to dovetail into one pure, joyful experience.

"You seem to draw your strength from this place," Al said as he looked out at the panoramic view in front of them.

They had hiked high up into the mountain behind her parent's house on a clear Sunday in August. The crystalline air, although warm with sunshine, felt faintly damp with the nearness of autumn. The rustling leaves of the aspens growing along the hill crest seemed to sigh with contentment. Lisl turned her face up to the sun and felt the warm breeze caress her. She sat serenely gazing at the horizon. Everything was green and growing and heavy with ripeness. The myriad of wildflowers were lush with color and texture — the delicate pinks of a wild rose, the velvety petals of a giant poppy, or the translucent pale green of the mountain bellflower. Lisl delighted in it all, and she wanted Al to love it, too.

He stood awkwardly now on the slope of the hill regarding her with a quizzical look, "I've never seen you more at peace than up here. You're really in your element, aren't you?"

"This is where I used to come as a child to sort out life's little problems. I called it my secret place. Whenever Mama got angry with me, I'd run off and come up here. I was convinced that no one would ever find me, but each time Mama sent Anne or Frieda up here to get me. They knew right where to find me every time — I guess I wasn't fooling anyone," she said with a laugh. "I suppose I love it so much because my roots are here, Al. This is where I grew up."

"Then I'm sure it'll be doubly hard for you to leave it when I get transferred back to the States," Al said soberly.

His eyes clouded over for an instant as they both reflected on the inevitable — that moment of truth when Lisl would leave behind everything dear and familiar to her and venture out for the unknown. The thought of it was at once exhilarating and terrifying. She felt a jumble of confusion.

Shaking her head, she said, "I don't even want to think about that right now. Let's just enjoy ourselves today. Look how beautiful those marguerites are over there. I just want to pick an armload of them!"

"Come on, it's getting chilly. Let's head back to the house," Al suggested. "Your mother has dinner ready, I'm sure."

Eventually, Al decided to join the United States Air Force, and soon they were transferred to Erding Air Base. By now, military rules applying to base privileges had softened, and Lisl was able to shop at the commissary. Nevertheless, weekend trips home still had her father stocking their trunk with home-grown offerings. Summer dissolved into fall and fall turned into winter. The time to leave and embark on a new life in the States was drawing near.

One spring day in '51 — one year after their transfer to Erding, Al came home with his papers.

"Honey, we're shipping out — we've been stationed at Carswell Air Force Base in Fort Worth, Texas," he said with a rueful smile. "I know how hard it will be for you to leave your family and all, but you'll love Texas. It's wide, open and free — a terrific place to raise a family."

"Texas! Don't they have cowboys and Indians there?" she asked. Visions of wild heathens beating drums and wielding tomahawks filled her head.

"You've been watching too many Westerns at the base movie house," he laughed. "Honest, Honey," he said, slipping his arms around her waist, "it'll be wonderful."

Finally, the day Lisl had been dreading came. Base Housing sent movers to pack their personal belongings: the heirloom Rosenthal china her mother had given her, the lead crystal, silver and other accumulated valuables were all carefully wrapped and boxed. Their bags were packed; the furniture was crated and ready to be shipped by boat. Her entire family came to the Munich-Riem Airport to see them off.

Anita toddled around caught up in all the excitement, totally unaware of the enormity of the moment. As they waited in the airport restaurant, Lisl glanced up at the clock on the wall and thought, it's ticking much too fast. If only she could slow it down.

Finally they heard the flight called over the loudspeaker. Al somberly took her hand, "Honey, we need to go."

Michael slowly got up from his chair. Suddenly he seemed much older than his sixty-five years. His drawn face remained immobile, but his eyes showed the anguish that was in his heart. He came over to hug his youngest daughter good-bye while the tears slid slowly down his cheeks. Lisl held her father for the last time, and felt his trembling arms. She heard him say huskily, "Never forget that we love you."

Lisl moved from her mother and sisters hugging and kissing them all good-bye as if in a daze.

Her husband, promising everyone that they would be back for frequent visits, swept Anita up in his arms as they began to walk down the concourse to the waiting Pan Am Clipper.

As they approached the aircraft, Anita turned to look over her daddy's shoulder and waved "bye-bye" to the sad little group they were leaving behind. As they boarded the plane, the piped-in music playing softly in the background was the song *"Auf Wiedersehen."*

Lisl stared out the window through her tears. On the observation deck her little family stood huddled together. Her three sisters were brushing tears away with one hand and waving white handkerchiefs with the other. Her mother stood amongst them smiling bravely and waving her hand. Lisl's eyes moved to the lone figure of her father standing slightly apart from the rest. His back was turned to them, his head was hanging down, and his shoulders were silently heaving. Lisl turned away from the window and looked at Al, her eyes welling with tears.

"I'll never see them again," she whispered in anguish as the tears streamed down her face. She felt as if her heart would break. Nothing in all of her traumatic wartime experiences compared to the utter and complete sadness that engulfed her at this moment. Anita, sensing that something was wrong with her mother, began to whimper. Lisl once again realized that she had to be brave — to be strong, as *Herr* Kohler put it so long ago "to be a good soldier" — if not for herself, then at least for the child that she was now responsible for. She quickly took the toddler in her arms and soothed her fears.

"It's going to be all right, Sweetheart. We're going to the United States. It'll all be wonderful and new," she crooned to her daughter through her tears. "Mommy is going to be all right." She looked around at the luxurious surroundings of the aircraft as she rocked the little girl in her lap. Al had told her a little about this airplane a few weeks ago, but at the time, she had been too distraught over the move to listen to all the details. Now in an effort to distract her, Al was pointing out some of the unique features of the airplane. "See those bunks overhead? This is the only passenger aircraft of its kind with these sleeping compartments. And that stairway over there? Guess where it leads to?"

Lisl shook her head.

"That leads up to the cocktail lounge! Isn't that amazing? This plane weighs forty-one tons and can carry over one hundred people!

With a hull of 109 feet long, it's one of the largest passenger planes around. It's called a Clipper because the earlier models of a few years ago actually landed on water! The problem with that was they could only land at an airport on a coast so passengers could transfer easily from a regular flight airplane to this one and vice versa. Just look at the plush carpeting, the curtains — isn't this luxurious?"

Lisl smiled through her tears and nodded. She tried to show interest in everything Al was saying, but her heart just wasn't in it.

As the plane began its slow ascent into the clouds, Lisl held her daughter in her arms rocking her gently to sleep. Smelling the sweet baby scent of her hair, she thought to herself, maybe Mommy *is* going to be all right. I have to pull myself together. I have a wonderful husband and daughter, she thought, and together, we're headed for a new life, in a new home, in a new country. The United States and Texas, in particular, sounded terribly exciting — fresh and new for her young family. A smile touched Lisl's lips as Irene's Meiers's words echoed from the distant past: "May God bless you and keep you well" Yes, Lisl thought, she was truly lucky to be alive.

EPILOGUE

The plane touched down on the runway with several short screeches, then taxied slowly to the terminal as the flight attendant thanked everyone, first in German and then in English, for flying Lufthansa and bid them all farewell.

Lisl wondered what changes in her homeland she would encounter on this sentimental journey, forty-five years after her first departure. It had been so long since she had been back to Germany, and so much had happened in the meantime. Yes, she had been back for a few visits, once when her mother fell ill, and then later, several times with Al and Anita. But, in the course of time, both her parents, all three of her sisters and their husbands had died. Lisl's father, Michael, had died within six months after her departure from Germany in '51. The stomach cancer he'd battled before had come back with a vengeance, and everyone said he had given up the will to live after the loss of his youngest daughter.

Lisl herself was a widow now, her beloved Al having succumbed to cancer sixteen years ago. The only living relatives left to her now in Germany were her nieces and nephews and, of course, their children and grandchildren. I'm the only one of my generation left, she thought sadly. The great-grand aunt of them all. Who will I be reunited with? She, who had always been the baby in the family, was now the matriarch. Still, it would be interesting to see the places she had told Anita about so often. And, she supposed, it was important for Anita to maintain her roots with these people. It was the place of *her* birth as well.

As the two women made their way through the baggage claim area, they could see a small welcome party waiting for them behind the glass partition — nieces and nephews as well as their spouses and a handful of small children — all smiling and waving huge bouquets of flowers. So many people! They had *all* come out to meet them! After joyous hugs, tearful kisses and everyone talking at once, they all piled into three cars and headed for Altmannstein. Lisl and Anita were to stay with Anne's daughter Marianne and her husband Martin who were now living in the same house that Anne and Ludwig had lived in so long ago.

"My, look at all the new houses!" Lisl remarked as they turned the familiar bend leading into Altmannstein.

"Those aren't new, *Tante* Lisl, they're the same old houses, just newly renovated," answered Marianne. How much she resembles her mother! thought Lisl, as she listened to Marianne's animated conversation. Even down to her mannerisms!

"All these houses you see here are now owned by the children of the people you grew up with, and they've taken great pride in renovating them," added Martin as he drove slowly through the town.

The little boy sitting between Lisl and Anita in the back seat looked up at the older woman and said shyly, "*Tante* Lisl, I colored this picture for you."

"Oh, Sasha, aren't you sweet!" Lisl was impressed with the polite manners of the little eight-year-old child. It was hard to believe he was Marianne's grandchild! How time passes, she thought.

Later, after an incredibly rich noontime meal of roast goose and gravy-soaked potato dumplings, Lisl and Anita took a short nap to fight off the jet lag that was already beginning to plague them.

"Well, some things never change, do they, Mother?" Anita said as they unpacked their suitcases. "Believe it or not, I vaguely remember this house."

"Oh, how could you? You were only two when we left!" her mother admonished.

"I know. I know. But something's very familiar about it all… I don't know, I can't put my finger on it."

Everyone rose early the next morning. Marianne and Martin

were going to take them on a whirlwind trip to all the old places Lisl and Anita had expressed an interest in seeing — Desching, where the munitions factory had been; Erding where the air base had been, and, of course, Regensburg. Everywhere they went, Lisl was awed by the flourishing prosperity and newness that surrounded her. The spanking clean buildings and shiny new cars all reflected the country's strong economy.

"We'll stop and eat lunch in Regensburg," Martin suggested, "I know of a wonderfully posh hotel there that serves the best smoked salmon."

"That'll be nice," Lisl said. She had been wrapped up in her own thoughts and hadn't paid too much attention to the chatter from the front seat. As they got out of the car and headed for the entrance to the luxury hotel, Lisl looked up at the sign on the building. In elegantly carved lettering the words: "The Golden Swan" towered overhead.

"The Golden Swan..." Lisl said slowly as she smiled to herself, "...The Golden Swan."

"Why, do you know this place?" asked Marianne.

"You could say that," she said quietly, "I ran by here once — a long time ago." Lisl was reminded of an old song, something about everything old being new again. But it was more than that, she felt. It was as if her past, like The Golden Swan, rose out of the ashes of war, and, with love and courage, survived to live a new day. She put her arm around Anita and said, "Come on, everybody, let's go in and eat."

Anita smiled at her mother and whispered, "Welcome home."